The Cape Coral Casanova

Murder on Crimson Court

Carol Freeman

To Mom, who taught me to live life to the fullest...

ACKNOWLEDGMENTS

A heartfelt thanks to Bill, my husband, my best friend, and once again, my partner in crime. His love and unwavering belief in me have been invaluable. Throughout our collaboration, he challenged me when I needed it and cheered me on when I deserved it. I am very grateful for his wild ideas and practical advice--even if I accepted his critique less than graciously, at times.

Carol Brott's support, straight-forward honesty, and literary expertise have helped me fine-tune this work. I greatly appreciate all her efforts from editing to promoting.

Tom Brott has, once again, designed a spectacular cover. Tom's artistic eye and meticulous work is very apparent. A special thank-you to Tom for his effort and patience.

Cathy and Buz, dear friends, have joined Carol and Tom in thoroughly embracing the spirit of the Bird-Watchers. In fact, the four of them have transformed themselves into the characters they inspired. Fiction has become reality.

I am very grateful to my children, Tamara and Brian. Each, in their own way, has taught me to take myself seriously as an author. Their encouragement and support have touched me deeply.

And, finally, I wish to extend my appreciation to the entire Cape Coral community. Their enthusiasm and warmth has overwhelmed Bill and me. They will always have a special place in our hearts. Thank-you, Cape Coral!

Carol Freeman

Prologue

Saturday, February 23

Saturday mornings in Cape Coral revolved around the Farmers' Market. The downtown market truly is the epicenter of this vibrant community. Families strolled around with their toddlers and pets in tow. A miniature pig on a leash snorted its way through the market, barely rating a glance from passersby. Vendors offered everything from ten-minute wrinkle reductions to produce, baked goods, hand-crafted jewelry, metal ibises, golf clubs, flip-flops, cheeses, stone crabs to a crowd teeming with local residents and snowbirds. However, today the market was visibly more animated and packed than ever before. A palpable energy reverberated all the way from the chili dogs to the goat cheese.

Ellen and Charlie, seventy-one-year-old snowbirds, couldn't wait to eat their way around the market. And they were ready, armed with large canvas bags and voracious appetites. This was their first foray into the market since last March. "Charlie, you get in line for almond croissants and I'll head right over to the pickle man," Ellen directed. "Meet you at the watermelons."

Ellen tried to wriggle by strollers toting around cockapoos, toy pugs, and, occasionally, a baby. Women wearing everything from spandex to muumuus were charging, en masse, towards a music tent set up in a corner at the far side of the market. Ellen was propelled forward by the crowd. She just clutched her canvas bag and hoped for the best. The pickle man would have to wait.

The decibel level shot upwards as the main act, wearing his guitar across his chest, stepped onto the temporary platform. "Hi, there, everyone," he smiled shyly. "You're b-e-a-u-t-i-f-u-l!" The women, all of them around Ellen's age, shrieked with delight. Arthritic knees jumped up and down with excitement. Shrill, fingers-in-the-mouth whistling hit high C.

Ellen tugged at the sleeve of the octogenarian next to her and shouted into her ear, "Who is this guy?"

"You don't know?" she replied incredulously. Ellen shook her head. "He's Cooper."

"Cooper who?"

"Just Cooper. And I think I'm in love with him," she swooned.

Taken aback by that comment, Ellen felt compelled to check out this sensation named 'Cooper'. He was probably in his early fifties, broad shouldered, lean, wearing tight jeans and a white tee shirt. With a practiced intensity, his eyes slowly scanned his adoring fans. But it was his smile that captivated the hearts of these women. Cooper had a way of tilting his head, ever so slightly, letting his smile lazily emerge. As he began to play his guitar and sing The Temptations "My Girl", a lock of his thick, salt and pepper hair covered his right eye. By the time the song ended, the post-menopausal crowd was shouting and clapping, "Michelle, MICHELLE, M-I-C-H-E-L-L-E!"

Opening up his arms, Cooper cocked his head and surrendered to the will of his groupies. Suddenly, the crowd became so quiet, Ellen could hear herself swallowing. Then, Cooper hugged his guitar, played the intro, and began to croon the Beatles' "Michelle", his signature song. Cooper ended his iconic appearance with Neil Diamond's "Song Sung Blue".

Modestly lowering his head, he thanked the crowd for their support. "I am humbled by your love. Remember that your beauty knows no age." He paused, smiling as he invoked his fans, "Please join me." They all chanted his mantra in unison, "AND AGE IS NOT A NUMBER!"

Ellen reluctantly broke away and found Charlie.

"So, what was all that commotion about?" Charlie inquired. "You seemed to be in the thick of it."

"Cooper," Ellen said.

"What?"

"Cooper," she repeated.

"What?" Charlie asked, perplexed.

"Just Cooper, Charlie," Ellen replied glibly. She was, contentedly, singing "My Girl" to herself as they headed over to the pickle man.

The adoring fans had not a clue that they had witnessed, what was to be Cooper's final performance.

One Day Earlier

Friday, February 22

Ellen and Charlie Green arrived in Cape Coral, Florida for their six-week stay. A sunny, eighty-five-degree day greeted them. They were ecstatic that they had made their getaway from Montgomery, NY just before the latest Nor'easter struck, and, immensely pleased with their fortuitous timing.

Having mastered the art of snowbirding, Ellen and Charlie knew how to quickly settle into the Airbnb house on Wisteria Court that they rented every winter. Their basic plan was that Ellen would carry their personal items into the house while Charlie would pile up, in the garage, all the antiques that they had purchased at the Mount Dora Antique Extravaganza. Ellen and Charlie were antique dealers who rented space in the Barn at Water Street Market back home in New Paltz, NY. On their way to Cape Coral, they made an annual pilgrimage to Mount Dora to replenish their inventory.

Of course, this plan was heavily dependent on Charlie, who provided the muscle. From years of lifting and hauling cupboards, planters, statues, typewriters, and other ridiculously heavy items, Charlie looked and acted a decade younger than his seventy-one years. His six-foot two-inch frame, broad shoulders and mischievous glint in his eye could still make Ellen blush.

Yet, by late afternoon, Charlie was wiping the sweat from his eyes. His legs felt like concrete weights. He peered into the back of his Ford Transit and saw one remaining item. He could swear that it was mocking him: a damn jelly cupboard. Charlie heaved a heavy sigh and slid the cupboard to the edge of the van. He managed to maneuver the bottom of the cupboard onto the driveway. He left it propped up against his van.

"Hey, Ellen, could you come out here? I could use a little help," Charlie yelled in a rare surrender to his age. Ellen did not respond. Charlie called to her several more times with no response.

Ellen did not respond because, unbeknownst to Charlie, she had gone AWOL. She had headed down the street to check out a yard sale. Ellen couldn't wait to show Charlie her treasures. She was weighted down carrying a funky chandelier, two tool boxes, a watering can and a Smith-Corona typewriter. Approaching the driveway, she called out, "Charlie, wait till you see what I bought!"

When Ellen saw the cupboard leaning on the van and no Charlie, she dropped her stuff on the lawn and began frantically shouting, "Charlie! Charlie!" No response. She knew that Charlie was too stubborn to leave a cupboard propped up and just walk away from it. Something was terribly wrong. Ellen continued to call to Charlie as she ran from the driveway to the garage to the house. No response. By now, she was imagining that Charlie had keeled over and was lying unconscious on the floor of the lanai. The lanai was empty. There was still no sign of Charlie.

As she looked out to the canal from the lanai, Ellen squinted. She thought she spied the top of a navy blue baseball cap down by the dock. She dashed to the dock and was greeted with, "Hi there, Ellen. Care to join me?"

Charlie was seated at a patio table, legs splayed out in total relaxation. In his right hand was a can of Coors Light.

"Oh, my God, Charlie, I thought you were dead!" Ellen cried out in relief.

"Ellen, Sweetie, I'm fine," Charlie reassured her. He looked up at Ellen. Her trim figure and tendency to scoot never failed to make Charlie stop and stare just like he did twenty-five years ago. "Look, my knee buckled twice under me while I was unloading that van. So, I've decided to start acting my age, for a change."

"Not a bad idea," Ellen agreed. They both sat quietly and enjoyed doing nothing for a few minutes.

Since it was already late afternoon, Ellen and Charlie decided that shopping for food could wait until tomorrow. Instead, they opted for drinks and a sunset at the Boat House. The Boat House Tiki Bar and Restaurant was situated at Redfish Point right on the beach, adjacent to the fishing pier.

The locals and tourists all vied for a seat on the rail, overlooking the water. And, the place was packed, as always. Ellen strutted in with confidence. She was certain that any of the servers would gladly shove people aside in order to give them premiere seating. After all, last winter she and Charlie had solved the murder on the Caloosahatchee River. Much to Ellen's disappointment, only one server noticed them and that was because he was carrying a tray filled with drinks and couldn't get past Ellen. "Excuse me!" the server generically shouted. Ellen glared at him and Charlie swiftly steered her away. The unsuspecting server had no idea that by ignoring Ellen he invited a verbal monsoon.

Fortunately, at that instant, they heard someone shout, "Charlie, Ellen! Welcome back!" It was Colleen, the assistant manager, whose fun-loving spirit made every customer feel special. Colleen quipped, "Do you realize that since you went up North, every single person who has walked out onto the pier has made it back alive?"

Ellen laughed, "Well, we'll have to do something about that. How have you been, Colleen?"

"Fantastic! And you, two, look great. When did you arrive?"

"About three hours ago. We rushed down here just to see you and, well, while we're here, we figured we might as well check out the sunset," Charlie winked.

"Well, Charlie, I see you haven't changed a bit!" Colleen teased as she headed over to talk to one of the bartenders.

Charlie gently guided Ellen to the railing for a view of the beach, the water, and the crimson ball of fire getting ready to disappear beyond the horizon.

They walked onto the beach and strolled, hand-in-hand, down the entire length of the pier where, one year ago, Jack Newman had been murdered.

Much later that evening, Ellen and Charlie had no intention of going to bed without observing their nightly ritual: the hot tub. They ambled onto the spacious lanai, marveling as the underwater hot tub lights dramatically changed colors. Charlie poured each of them a glass of sauvignon blanc and they climbed in. The jets of warm water soothed their minor aches and officially ushered in their winter vacation. Charlie proposed a toast. "Here's to a relaxing and uneventful winter."

Reaching out to clink glasses with Charlie, Ellen lost her balance and spilled most of her wine. "Hope that isn't an omen," she laughed. "To a relaxing and uneventful winter!"

The Soledad Country Club was hosting senior mixed doubles tennis this morning. Beverly Miller was playing at the net and had just slammed the ball at her opponents, winning the next point. She was confident that she and her partner, Herb, would win the match. They just needed one more point. Instead, Herb had the misfortune to double fault, earning Beverly's silent wrath. After the obligatory handshake with the winners, Beverly said good-bye and headed to her white Buick. She was annoyed that Herb was such a sloppy player. At seventy-eight, he was ten years younger than she but moved like an old man. Beverly, on the other hand, never wasted a step and rarely wasted her time. From now on, Herb would have to find another partner for mixed doubles. Checking her watch, she realized that she had barely enough time to shower and return for the women's luncheon.

An hour later, Beverly walked onto the patio where the luncheon was to take place. Her erect posture and purposeful gait made her appear taller than she actually was. "Hey, Beverly! Over here," called her friend, Phyllis.

Beverly nodded and made her way to Phyllis' table. "So, tell me again, Phyllis. What is this fund-raiser all about?"

"It's about Cooper," she replied.

"Cooper?"

"Oh, Beverly, he's the hot singer I was telling you about. Anyhow, he's trying to raise money to open up a music studio strictly for seniors. And, right here in Cape Coral! We'll be able to take lessons, be in a band--you name it."

"That's considered a charitable cause?" Beverly grumbled.

"I'm just saying that once you hear him and, even better, once you see him, you'll understand," Phyllis winked. "Besides," Phyllis whispered, "I entered each of us in the raffle."

"And what do we get if we win? An arrangement of plastic daisies?"

"Beverly, no. The winner gets a dinner date with Cooper!"

Before Beverly could groan back, the Soledad Ladies' League chair addressed the women. "Welcome, everyone. This is an exciting day for the Soledad Ladies' League. First, I'd like to thank you all for your generous donations." The chair paused to take a deep breath. "After our --ahem--main act," she tittered, "we will be announcing the winner of the raffle. But, without further ado, I present someone who needs no introduction: COOPER!"

Sixty country club ladies began to cheer, "C-O-O-P-E-R!

C-O-O-P-E-R!" Beverly applauded politely.

"Lovely ladies," Cooper began, tilting his head as his smile slowly spread. He crooned and charmed his way through his repertoire, ending with Frank Sinatra's "I've Got You Under My Skin". The room quieted down as soon as Cooper spoke into the mic and said, "Thank-you, ladies. And, remember that your beauty knows no age.

10

And," pausing to spread out his arms and invite his fans to join him, "AGE IS NOT A NUMBER!" the room exploded in unison.

"And, now, Cooper will draw the name of the lucky lady who will go to dinner with him tomorrow!" squealed the Chair.

Cooper dramatically reached into the bowl of tickets, swished them around a bit, closed his eyes and retrieved one lucky name. "And, my dinner date will be," he said with a twinkle in his eye, waiting several seconds to build tension, "Beverly Miller. Come on up here, Beverly Miller!"

Beverly felt her face redden with embarrassment. She wished she had never agreed to attend this ridiculous luncheon. Slowly, she stood up and made her way to the front of the room. Before she had a chance to protest, Cooper swept her up in a big hug. The crowd cheered. Cooper waved and made his exit. Beverly strutted back to her seat.

All of a sudden, gushing and bursting with excitement, the entire Soledad Ladies' League surrounded Beverly. "Hah!" she thought to herself, "They're jealous as hell!" She smiled benevolently at the other women, all of them pretending to be happy for her.

On this particular Sunday, Cooper had a busy schedule. He was expected to attend another fund-raiser at an exclusive golf club in Fort Myers early that evening. Therefore, it was late Sunday night when he finally arrived at Maya Wolfson's apartment. Maya had been working for Cooper as his sound-tech. Their relationship had been strictly a business relationship, that is, until very recently. Nevertheless, it continued to be a business relationship, which greatly complicated matters. Tonight, though, was pure lust.

Two hours later, Maya quickly threw on an oversized tee shirt and walked Cooper to his car without bothering to put on shoes. They stood in front of the car in a lingering embrace. Any casual passerby would immediately recognize them as new lovers.

Monday, February 25

Beverly played Monday morning tennis with the same group just as she always did on Monday mornings. On her drive home, she thought about how satisfying it was that she and her partner had won their match. Today's match had been challenging. However, Beverly was equally delighted that her tennis friends all rushed over to greet her, buzzing about her upcoming dinner date. As the winner of the dinner-with-Cooper raffle, Beverly was instantly elevated to celebrity status. She rose to her new standing effortlessly, assuming an air of superiority. She promised to hold court at breakfast on Tuesday to "tell all".

As soon as Beverly pulled into her parking space at her condo, her phone rang. "Hi, Laura."

"Hi, Mom. Sorry I didn't return your call last night. Everything okay? You sounded agitated."

Beverly laughed and said, "Laura, everything is fine. Wonderful, in fact! I've got some exciting news for you."

"Yes?" Laura inquired.

"I've got a hot date tonight."

"You, what? Mom? What are you talking about?"

"I won a raffle and won a dinner date with this singer, Cooper."

"Never heard of him."

13

"Well, he's a big deal down here, especially among us women of a certain age, my dear," Beverly explained.

"Mom, what do you really know about him?"

"Laura, nothing. Nothing at all and I don't care. Do you realize I've become the envy of every woman over sixty? I practically got a standing ovation at tennis this morning. I intend to make the most of this!"

"Mom!"

"Laura, dear, I really have to hang up now. I've got to figure out what to wear this evening and I need time to shave my legs."

"Mom!" But Beverly had already ended the call.

Laura knew that her mother was no helpless little old lady, but she was eighty-eight and sounded like a rebellious teenager. Laura was worried and knew exactly what she had to do.

Ellen was preparing for a busy day of, well, doing as little as possible. She carried a book, her phone, and a chair down to the dock out back. She snapped a couple of photos of the picturesque view of neighbors' boats neatly tied up along the entire length of the canal. Many of the residential streets backed up to canals. In fact, Cape Coral is a city with four hundred miles of canals, making it the city with the most miles of navigable waterways in the world. Ellen was about to sit down when her phone "can-canned", her default ringtone. It was her friend, Ginger, from back home in Montgomery. "Hi, Ginger! Good to hear from you."

"Hi, Ellen. How is Cape Coral? Wait, don't tell me. I really do not want to hear about it," Ginger said.

"Well, then, I won't say a word. But whatever you're imagining it's like, it's even better!" Ellen couldn't resist taunting.

"And whatever you're imaging Montgomery is like right about now, it's even worse!"

"How's Hugh?"

"You know. The same. Right now he's snow-blowing the driveway in his goggles, windbreaker, and neon yellow bathing suit just to shock the neighbors. Look, Ellen, I have a favor to ask of you."

"Sure. Ask away."

"A Garden Club friend of mine, Laura, is concerned about her mother who happens to live in Cape Coral."

"What's going on with her mother?"

"This may sound a bit weird, but her mother is eighty-eight years old and is all hyped-up about going on a dinner date with some singer, Cooper."

"A date with Cooper?" Ellen asked incredulously.

"Yes. It seems she won a raffle and he was the grand prize."

15

Ellen laughed, "Well, Ginger, Cooper seems to be the hot ticket here. Woman are orgasmic over this guy!"

"Anyhow, Laura would really appreciate your reaching out to her mother to make sure her virginity is still intact after this date."

"No problem," Ellen giggled. "Text me her name and address. I'll take it from there and get back to you."

"Thanks, Ellen. I knew Laura could count on you. Regards to Charlie."

"And to Hugh. Speak to you soon!"

By dinnertime, Ellen and Charlie were looking forward to half-price pizza night at Maria's. Maria's Pizzeria and Restaurant has been a Cape Coral favorite for almost thirty years. To this day, Maria's still uses the old family recipes that continue to be so popular.

Every Monday, for the last twelve years or so, Catherine, Charlie's sister-in-law, and her husband Ted have gone to Maria's Pizzeria and Restaurant. They had been living in Cape Coral for fifteen years and were the driving force that lured Ellen and Charlie to Cape Coral each year. Catherine is a retired educator. Ted is an avid and talented photographer, winning national awards for his bird photographs. They were always joined by their friends Karen and Bud. The two couples had been friends for over forty years, sharing life's highs and lows. Bud is a retired NYC fire fighter. Karen is a retired nurse. Karen and Bud had moved to Cape Coral many years ago and didn't have to work hard to convince Catherine and Ted to join them. They all included Ellen and Charlie in their weekly tradition, embracing the new arrivals as extended family.

Ruth, the owner, rushed over to give Ellen and Charlie a hearty greeting as soon as they entered. "Great to see my favorite snowbirds! How have you been?"

"Ruth, wonderful to see you! We've been great. And you?" Ellen asked.

Ruth nodded and said, "Good. You know, just the usual craziness," gesturing with her head, to the overflowing crowd waiting to be seated.

Charlie added, "We sure have missed you!" Ruth smiled and escorted them to the round table where their friends were waiting.

"Hey, good to see you!" Charlie called, opening up his arms to give them each a big hug.

"Well, it's about time," Catherine greeted them.

Bud muttered, "Let's just see if, this year, we can have a normal, stress-free couple of months. No more murders, please."

They all toasted in unanimous agreement. But, while they waited for their pizzas to arrive, they amused themselves reminiscing about last year's zany adventure.

Beverly made sure to arrive at the Boat House a few minutes late for breakfast so she could make an entrance. She paraded over to the big table where her tennis group had gathered. She was prepared to treat this like a press conference.

"So, come on, Beverly," Phyllis pleaded. "Tell us about last night!"

Beverly took the seat saved for her at the head of the table. Everyone was silently waiting for her to spill her guts. "Well," she began, "he showed up with a dozen red roses. Then, we got in his car and drove to Redfish Point Grill for dinner."

"Ooh!" the women swooned at the mention of Redfish Point Grill. This restaurant is known for its steak and seafood, its excellent service, and its lovely courtyard.

"We sat in a quiet corner of the courtyard, hidden by tropical plants, and had a fantastic dinner."

"What did you have?" asked one woman.

"I had the crab cakes and they did it right. Fresh crabmeat without all that filler."

"Who cares what you had," grumbled another. "I just want to know what Cooper is really like."

"That's right. Did he sing to you?" another tennis friend asked breathlessly.

Beverly fielded all the questions like a true professional. When she was asked if he tried "to get in her pants," she replied with a haughty look and said, "He was a perfect gentleman."

By mid-afternoon Ellen decided to put down her book and check up on Ginger's friend's elderly mother, Beverly Miller. So, she drove to Miramar Court, only a few blocks away. Ellen rang the bell and expected to wait, knowing that at eighty-eight, shuffling to answer the door was going to take Beverly some time. Instead, Ellen was startled that, almost immediately, a husky voice demanded to know who was at the door.

"Hi, Beverly. I'm Ellen Green," Ellen shouted. "Your daughter, Laura, wanted me to stop by. I live up North in Montgomery, NY."

"You might as well come in," Beverly replied, opening the door. "Laura thinks I've gone loopy. That's why you're here. Right?"

Ellen nodded. Beverly had closely cropped, white hair and was wearing a tee-shirt that read, "I'VE GOTTA BE ME ". Her athletic stance and her air of confidence was a bit intimidating, even to Ellen.

"Ellen, would you like some iced tea?"

"I'd love some. Thanks."

"So, Laura put you up to this?"

"'Fraid so, Beverly. You frightened her when you said you had a hot date with Cooper."

"Well, I did have a hot date. So?" Beverly retorted, handing Ellen a glass of iced tea.

"Thank-you. Your friends must all be jealous," Ellen deduced with a wry smile.

Beverly raised one eyebrow and replied, "Well, wouldn't you be?"

Ellen couldn't deny that, having experienced Cooper on Saturday. "He does have that ability to make a woman feel special," she whispered.

"I must say, I was a skeptic, but Cooper was charming."

"And," Ellen added, "very sexy."

"He was the perfect gentleman," Beverly replied.

She and Ellen chatted for a few more minutes before Beverly decided to get right to the point. "So, what do you plan to say to Laura?"

"That her mother is one smart, lucky babe!"

"Thanks for checking up on the dottering old lady, but I don't have time to chat. I have to get ready for my poker game tonight. See you," Beverly said abruptly.

"A pleasure to meet you, Beverly."

On this balmy night, Cooper had enjoyed an evening at Fathoms, located at Cape Harbour Marina. Both the patio seating at the restaurant and the open-air bar overlooked the expansive marina. Cooper chose to sit outside at the bar, where he had a couple of beers and ordered a pizza. His baggy sweats and baseball cap provided enough of a disguise that he was not recognized. It was a relief to be anonymous and just be Mark Simmons from Indianapolis, again. For the last year, every part of his life was a sham. He, even, maintained a rundown studio apartment in Cape Coral, solely, to establish his bohemian and bare-bones lifestyle. Part of his public persona. "But," he chuckled to himself, "it's all been worth it."

Cooper was taking pleasure in the short walk home to his penthouse. He looked forward to drinking a martini and stretching out on his screened-in lanai. From that vantage point, he could practically see all the way to Sanibel Island. As he turned right off El Dorado Parkway onto Crimson Court, he was greeted by an impressive canopy of twenty-foot tall poinciana trees. These trees have a dense foliage that spreads outward, providing welcome shade to locations in south Florida. Crimson Court was named for the brilliant red blossoms that burst forth from these trees every spring. Walking by this shaded canopy always soothed Cooper, no matter how chaotic his day had been. The trees were a comforting sight. They meant that he was almost home.

Cooper was singing Billy Joel's "Uptown Girl", snapping his fingers, and walking down the street at a jaunty pace. He heard footsteps coming up from behind him and was amused that they were almost in step with his own. They strode down the street in tandem for a few beats before Cooper heard his name being called. He whipped around in response and was face-to-face with raw anger.

21

At that instant, in Cooper's mind, everything shifted into a hazy, slow motion. He was confident that he could still charm his way out of this precarious situation. He knew he was a virtuoso at winning over, even, the most formidable adversary. Maybe smile and offer to buy a drink at Fathoms. Yeah, that'll do it. Unfortunately, Cooper discovered, too late, that his charm had, indeed, failed him when he needed it the most. Without warning, it was a clean, fast-forward thrust, as the knife found its way deep into Cooper's heart.

Wednesday, February 27

This morning, Charlie was enjoying his two-mile walk to the beach, nodding and greeting everyone he encountered along the way. Ellen had driven down, parked the car, and was briskly jogging her way through the Yacht Club neighborhood. When they met up at the Boat House for coffee, they saw all the customers gathered around the bar. Quietly, Ellen and Charlie joined the crowd to see what all the excitement was about.

Charlie asked a guy at the bar, "What's going on?"

"Shhh!" was the response from a nearby customer.

A 'regular' at the other end of the bar continued to read from the Cape Coral Daily Breeze. "*Two women discovered the body alongside a poinciana tree just before midnight. He died from a stab wound. No weapon was found. The Cape Coral Police Department is asking anyone with information to contact their hotline at 239 624-3951.*"

"Who was murdered?" Ellen asked.

"You haven't heard?" someone answered.

"It was that guy, Cooper," a woman sipping coffee stated.

"What? The singer?" Ellen cried out.

"Yup."

Ellen leaned close and whispered, "Oh, my God, Charlie, we've got to get home! I need to visit Beverly Miller and see if she's okay. She had dinner with Cooper on Monday!"

"Fine. Check on her, but nothing more. You can't get involved in this, Ellen," Charlie warned. He was troubled to see an all-too familiar glimmer in Ellen's eye.

By late morning, Ellen arrived at Beverly Miller's home. She was surprised to see a line-up of Buicks and Lincolns parked near Beverly's house. She rang the bell and was greeted by someone who introduced herself as 'Phyllis'. "Hello, Phyllis. I'm Ellen. I heard the news about Cooper and wanted to see how Beverly was doing."

"As well as can be expected, under the circumstances," Phyllis replied somberly. "Come on in."

Ellen followed Phyllis onto the lanai and saw Beverly seated, surrounded by seven or eight of her friends. The women made a path, allowing her access to Beverly. Ellen wasn't sure whether she was expected to genuflect or kiss her ring. Instead, she bent down and gave Beverly a brief hug. "You okay?"

Beverly shrugged her shoulders and sighed. Phyllis filled in the silence. "Beverly is somewhat in a state of shock from the news. But, we're all here for her." Beverly blew her nose loudly, honking in appreciation.

"So, how do you know Beverly?" asked one of the friends.

Before Ellen could respond, Beverly chimed in, "Ellen is a snowbird from Montgomery, NY who came to check up on me yesterday. My daughter, Laura, seems to think I'm some demented old biddy!"

Ellen cleared her throat, hoping to disguise a laugh. One of the friends retorted, "Well, she obviously never had to face you on the tennis court!"

"Here, here!" they all raised their glasses and toasted in unison.

"Ellen, please join us for a gin and tonic," Phyllis offered, walking over to the bar and liberally pouring gin into a tall glass. Ellen took a sip and hoped that she could hold her own among these Beefeater babes.

Soon the bantering took a subdued turn as conversation shifted to Cooper. The more they drank, the more they sobbed. The more they sobbed, the more they drank. Ellen decided to leave while she could still find her way home. She waved, told Beverly she'd be in touch, and headed in the direction of the front door.

The doorbell rang and Phyllis staggered over to answer it. She, clearly, saw herself as Beverly's personal sentinel. Ellen stepped aside so the man at the door could enter. "Raul!" Ellen exclaimed, taken aback. Raul Swann was the young police detective Ellen and Charlie had befriended last year. Raul had been, alternately, frustrated, concerned, and impressed by these outrageous snowbirds.

"Ellen Green?" Raul replied, startled. "So, you're back in Cape Coral, I see."

Ellen replied with a big hug. She thought that Raul still looked young enough to have acne rather than facial hair. "Yes. Just arrived on Friday. And how are you enjoying life as a sergeant?"

"Trying to do my job. By the way, how's Charlie?"

"He's great. And Jennifer?"

"Actually, Jennifer and I are pregnant. She's due in September."

"Raul, congratulations!"

"Thanks, Ellen. Now, I need to ask you what you're doing here."

Ellen gave an innocent shrug as she explained, "Just checking up on a friend's, friend's mother. Nothing more, Raul. Why?"

"Really, Ellen. There happens to have been another murder here in Cape Coral--in fact, the only murder since you were here last-- and you happen to turn up in the home of the woman who had dinner with the victim the night before he was killed." Raul folded his arms across his chest and waited for Ellen to say something.

Ellen always believed in taking the offensive. "And, I need to ask you what you're doing here. You don't really think that Beverly Miller had anything to do with Cooper's murder. Do you?"

"Look, Ellen, I'm doing my job." Raul Swann was one of those good-looking guys who didn't seem to know he was good-looking. His face softened and broke into a warm smile as he added, "And, you haven't changed a bit. It's good to see you again. Please give Charlie my best."

"And give Jennifer a hug from me."

"And, Ellen," Raul shook his finger at her, "please do not get involved in this investigation. I'm serious."

"Raul, " Ellen replied dismissively, "you know me better than that!"

That night, Ellen and Charlie's hot tub routine deviated slightly from their usual tradition: Ellen emphatically refused a glass of sauvignon blanc. She was still sobering up from her afternoon spree with the ladies. "But, Charlie, what do you think Raul was looking to find out from Beverly?"

"I'm sure he needs to interview everyone who had contact with Cooper recently. Beverly Miller was, probably, one name on a long list of people he had to see." Charlie threw his head back, closed his eyes, and took a slow, deep breath as the jets massaged his lower back.

"And, imagine what Raul must have thought when he stepped onto that lanai and realized he had to contend with a bevy of rowdy cougars," Ellen giggled.

"I wouldn't have a clue," Charlie replied with a smirk.

Thursday, February 28

Police headquarters was bustling at this early morning hour. Captain McConnell had summoned Raul's detective unit to a meeting. The half dozen police detectives were all seated at a conference table with Captain McConnell at one end and Detective Sergeant Raul Swann at the other. "Officers, good morning. Detective Sergeant Swann will be briefing us all on the status of the Cooper murder investigation. Swann, I turn the meeting over to you."

"Thank-you, Captain. Officers, the preliminary report from the coroner indicates that Cooper, A.K.A. Mark Simmons, died from a straight four-inch blade that pierced through the heart. The victim, fifty-two years old, was found, supine, alongside a poinciana tree within a block from his home on Crimson Court. Death is estimated to have occurred on Tuesday, February 26, between twenty-two hundred hours and twenty-three hundred hours. To date, no weapon has been found and no witnesses have come forward. The following items were found on his person: eight hundred dollars in denominations of twenty, a mobile phone, and a personal check made out to Cooper for five hundred dollars from a Beverly Miller, 5231 Miramar Court. Any questions so far?"

All the officers shook their heads. Sergeant Swann continued, "Here is the list of contacts from Cooper's phone. Every single person on that list needs to be interviewed by our unit. I will, personally, interview the contacts with an asterisk by the name. I need you to work with your partner and have all the interviews completed by Friday, sixteen-hundred hours. Is that clear?" Nods of agreement followed. "Thanks. Now, be safe, be smart, and be thorough."

From Fort Myers to Matlacha, women of a certain age and beyond were in various stages of grief and anger over the death of Cooper. Sharon Thompson was one of those women. She lived with her husband, Dr. Eli Thompson, proctologist, on Riverside Drive in a magnificent, contemporary home overlooking the Caloosahatchee. They enjoyed uninterrupted water views from every room in the house. Sharon and Eli often hosted sunset cocktail parties on the veranda to impress the Cape Coral elite.

This morning Sharon sat at the kitchen counter and quickly finished her third cup of black coffee. She only had an hour before a police detective was scheduled to arrive and she wanted to look her best. At sixty-five, Sharon worked hard not to look her age. Although her legs were still pretty shapely, her waist seemed to have disappeared completely. It was replaced by a slight, but distinct, equatorial bulge. As she checked her face in the mirror, she was horrified to see that her neck was beginning to resemble a turkey wattle. "Hmm, I've got to have something done about that!" Already, she could have fed an entire third-world country on what she spent each month for Botox, hair color touch-ups, yoga classes, facials, clothing, and make-up. She did not bother doing all this for Eli. He hadn't noticed her for, at least, a year now. They lived together in a perpetual state of hostile indifference. In fact, if it hadn't been for the check she wrote to Cooper's music studio fund, days would have gone by without him saying a single word to her.

Sharon thought back over the last month or so when she knew that Cooper was losing interest in her. He began backing out of their weekly luncheons with lame excuses. The more he backed away, the more desperate she became to hang onto him. The clandestine nature of the meetings was titillating for Sharon even though, regretfully, Cooper was never less than the perfect gentleman. And, then, a couple of weeks ago, in a frantic attempt to entice Cooper, Sharon wrote out a sizable check. In the past, she had donated to his fund in cash, so Eli never had to know about it. She knew she was being reckless, but she had no cash with her. She rationalized that Eli probably wouldn't even notice.

Sharon had miscalculated. Eli did notice. He discovered the check when he went online to pay for the National Proctologists' Convention that he attended each year. He flew into a rage and accused Sharon of having secret rendezvous with Cooper, which was true, but she denied it. Sharon accused Eli of caring only about the money, not her, which was true, but he denied that. Since their altercation, they have maintained an angry silence, not even acknowledging Cooper's murder.

A few minutes after 10:00 A.M., Detective Sergeant Raul Swann rang her doorbell. Pasting an inflated, red-lipped smile on her face, Sharon opened the door and was delighted to see a handsome, young detective smiling back at her. She invited him inside. After introductions, they sat in the kitchen with mugs of coffee for a few routine questions.

"Mrs. Thompson, your name came up as a contact on Cooper's mobile phone. So, first, let me extend my condolences to you."

"Thank-you, Detective."

"What was your relationship with Cooper?"

"I was one of his many female admirers," Sharon said simply.

"But why were you listed as one of his phone contacts?" Raul inquired, perplexed.

"Not sure," she replied. "Maybe it was because I donated, let's just say, rather generously to his music studio fund."

"What is this fund all about?"

"Cooper was passionate about opening up a music studio for seniors. He envisioned a venue where seniors could take lessons, perform together, even do some recording. He believed in his dream and I believed in him."

"And, how did you become familiar with his plans?"

"I had the good fortune of attending a fund-raising event at Southwest Tennis Club. Cooper performed and, well, by the time his performance ended, we women all waited in line to donate to his fund," she explained, seductively crossing her legs.

"But, Mrs. Thompson, why did he single you out? Not everyone there was a phone contact."

Sharon began fidgeting with her coffee mug. "I offered to host an event for him in my home. That's why."

"And, did you?"

"Did I what?" Sharon asked evasively.

"Did you host an event for Cooper in your home, here?"

Sharon sighed, stroking her wattle. "No, we hadn't scheduled anything yet."

Raul continued, "Please tell me what Cooper was like. I'm trying to get a handle on him."

"Cooper," she said clenching her jaw, "Cooper had a way of making women my age feel beautiful and," she paused, "well, sexy."

Raul nodded, not wanting to interrupt.

She flashed her thickly mascaraed eyes at Raul. "He was a true artist. He wasn't the greatest singer, but when he sang, every woman in the audience felt that he was singing for her, alone."

"Is that what you felt, too?"

"Are you kidding?" Sharon responded cynically. "I knew it was all an act. But, it was a convincing act. I will say that," she added with an edge to her voice.

"An act?"

"Yes, Detective. He knew how to charm us. We were all quite eager to make sizable donations."

"I see. When was the last time you had contact with Cooper, Mrs. Thompson?"

"Let me think," she mused. "Ah, I know. It was a couple of weeks ago. I wrote him a check--a donation to his fund--and presented it to him."

Raul looked at Sharon skeptically, "And, did your husband know of this donation?"

"Detective Swann, absolutely! We don't keep secrets from one another. And, besides, Eli is a very generous man. If it made me happy to donate, it made Eli happy," she smiled ambiguously.

Raul cleared his throat before he continued. "You said that you presented it to him. You mean, in person?"

Sharon could feel her face turning red as heat rose from her core. "I-I, um, I went to Cooper's apartment to leave it for him. When he wasn't there, I left it in his mailbox."

"Really? Where was his apartment?"

"Detective, I am quite sure that you already know the answer to that question and have searched the place with black lights and dusted for fingerprints!"

"Mrs. Thompson, I would appreciate your answering my question."

"Jackson Lane. One of those wretched little studio apartments. Not far from the Dollar Store."

Raul politely nodded and wrote that down on his notepad. "Just one more question, Mrs. Thompson. Where were you between 10:00 P.M. and 11:00 P.M. on Tuesday, February 26th?"

"I was home watching 'This is Us' on my iPad."

"Was anyone with you?"

"No, Detective. Is there anything else I can help you with?" Sharon asked impatiently, standing up to end the interview.

"Nothing at this time. Thank-you for your cooperation." Raul reached out to shake her hand. As he opened the front door to exit, he turned back to Sharon for one final comment. "Oh, I almost forgot. I meant to tell you that the Cooper Music Studio Fund never existed, Mrs. Thompson. I'm afraid, you've been had."

Sharon slammed the door so hard, the mirror in the front hall fell off the wall and shattered.

Friday, March 1

Charlie was seated at the bar at the Boat House waiting for Ellen to finish her morning run. "Hi, Amy!" he greeted his favorite server, giving her a hug.

"Charlie, great to see you! I didn't realize you and Ellen were back in Cape Coral."

"We got here a week ago and heard that you were on vacation. Good to see you, too."

Amy whispered, "You heard about the murder, I suppose."

Charlie nodded.

"I'm pretty freaked-out about it. I'll be right back with coffee for you and Ellen," Amy said as another customer signaled to get her attention.

An attractive woman in her early sixties, seated on Charlie's left, sidled closer to him. "We're *all* pretty freaked-out about the murder," she added softly. "This guy Cooper was really something! The older women loved him. He wasn't my type, but," she shrugged her shoulders, "to each his own, I suppose. By the way, I'm Stella and you are?"

"Charlie," he said reaching out to shake her hand as he saw Ellen approaching. "Ellen, how was your run?" Charlie stood up and greeted her with a kiss.

"It was good, Sweetie."

35

"Ellen, this is Stella." The women shook hands. "Stella and I were talking about the Cooper murder."

Ellen asked, "Did you know him?" Amy arrived with two coffees. "Amy! Great to see you again. Thanks for the coffee."

Ellen and Amy exchanged a quick hug and Amy winked, "This first one's on me, guys. Enjoy."

"Thanks, Amy!" Charlie smiled.

Ellen resumed her conversation with Stella. "So, did you know Cooper personally?"

"No, but I saw him perform right here at the Boat House one afternoon. The place was packed--and the crowd was all women."

"When was that?" Ellen asked.

"Let me see. I gave my neighbor, Mildred, a ride so she could hear him. Mildred was obsessed with Cooper!" Stella rolled her eyes. "So, that must have been a while ago. Hmmm. Maybe back in November, I think."

"Mildred must be taking his death very hard," Ellen surmised.

"Well, not really. She was in her early nineties and died just a few weeks ago."

"Oh, I'm sorry to hear that," Ellen said.

"Thanks. Mildred and I had been neighbors for many years. She was a little, you know, eccentric, but I really liked her."

"She was lucky to have you as a neighbor. Did Mildred have family living nearby?" Ellen asked.

"Just her son Frank. He rents a small place on El Dorado, near Chiquita Boulevard. I don't think she had any other children." Stella leaned in to talk, sotto voce, to Ellen and Charlie. "Actually, Frank was pretty angry when he learned that Mildred had changed her will very recently."

"What do you mean?" Ellen asked.

"Well, a few days after Mildred's funeral, Frank showed up at my door. I let him in and he started yelling at me, accusing me of pressuring Mildred."

Ellen and Charlie looked puzzled. Stella continued. "Right before Christmas, Mildred asked me to drive her to her attorney's office. I never like to meddle, so I didn't ask what it was about. Anyway, Frank seemed to think that I had something to do with a change in her will. The nerve!"

"Of course, you didn't," Ellen agreed. "So, what change did Mildred make?"

"You have to keep this between us." Ellen nodded vigorously. "Well, I could hardly believe this, myself, and I've seen and heard practically everything."

"Yes?"

"Well, I really shouldn't even be telling you this."

"Telling me what, Stella?" Ellen's limited patience was coming to a quick end.

"Well, turns out that Mildred left her entire estate to Cooper. Can you believe that?"

"She WHAT?" Ellen sputtered, dribbling coffee down the front of her tee shirt.

Charlie calmly asked, "Have you told this to the police?"

"Oh, no! I don't want to get involved in this."

"Stella, have you told anyone else about this?" Charlie asked.

"No. I've told no one. Please, please don't say anything."

Ellen smiled, "Don't worry, Stella. Oh, I forgot. What did you say Mildred's last name was, again?"

Charlie dreaded where Ellen was going with that question. "Sweetie, we need to get going. Remember, we're heading to Sanibel today."

"Blake," Stella replied. "Mildred Blake. She was a lovely woman."

"Yes, Charlie, you're right. We need to be on our way. Stella, good to meet you."

"Hope to see you here again," Charlie added.

"So glad to have met you, both."

Charlie climbed into the van and, before Ellen even closed her door, he said accusingly, "Ellen, who the hell do you think you're fooling? You were cross-examining that woman!"

"And, it's a good thing I did that," Ellen retorted.

"Ellen," Charlie pleaded, "you have to butt out of this. It's none of your business."

"But, Charlie, it is our business. Even Raul doesn't know about Mildred's will. All I want to do is ..."

"Ellen. No. I'm not getting involved--and neither are you!"

Ellen folded her arms across her chest and said nothing. She knew not to waste time arguing with Charlie. He was being pig-headed. But, a brief phone call to Catherine was in order. Catherine knew the back story about everything and everyone in Cape Coral. Ellen was confident that Catherine would come through with information about Mildred Blake.

Sanibel Island had a way of transcending petty disagreements. The breath-taking vistas over the Sanibel Causeway convinced every visitor that they were on their way to paradise. And, once they arrived, they were absolutely certain: this had to be paradise. This year, especially, Ellen and Charlie were eager to experience the raw beauty of this island nature preserve. They prided themselves on being able to bicycle from the lighthouse and Pinocchio's Ice Cream to Gene's Books at the opposite end. By the time they staggered over to Gene's Books, they met an author signing and selling his murder

39

mysteries that were set on Sanibel Island. Always intrigued by local authors, they gladly purchased a book. They pedaled back to Billy's Bicycles, refusing to succumb to fatigue or age-related aches. In fact, they, each, counted on the other one to yield first. And, neither ever did.

Although there was little visible evidence of destruction, the summer's red tide had had a devastating impact on fish and sea life. Over one hundred manatees and over three hundred sea turtles were killed by this toxic algae. The economy lost forty-one million dollars in revenue over the July to August period. This vulnerable island always seemed to rebound and become stronger: the Sanibel Island resilience.

Raul's day was consumed with the murder investigation. His unit was furiously gathering information about Cooper, but, in the meantime, a murderer was moving about freely. Tonight, though, he wanted to focus on Jennifer. He arrived home with a bouquet of daisies, produce from a farm stand, and two steaks. He was looking forward to preparing a wonderful dinner for the two of them to enjoy on the dock behind their house.

Raul had met Jennifer three years ago at a demonstration. A local restaurant owner had refused to seat a gay couple because they had kissed while waiting for their table. Once the words "faggot", "fairy", "pervert" started flying, pandemonium broke out. For the next two months, demonstrators picketed the restaurant to protest the owner's treatment of the gay couple. Jennifer was one of the demonstrators. Raul was one of the cops assigned to keep hostilities from escalating. When Jennifer attempted to enter the restaurant, he had to take action and stop her. Raul was instantly smitten.

Jennifer, an ob nurse, was still at work. So, Raul changed into a pair of shorts and a tee shirt and began preparing their dinner. By the time Raul began slicing cucumbers, he heard Jennifer's footsteps. "Hi, Honey! Sorry I'm so late. Had to help the doctor deliver a set of twins!"

Raul scooped her up in a big hug. He was still smitten.

"Well, that was some greeting! I think I'm going to be late more often," Jennifer said playfully. She grabbed a cucumber slice and sat on the kitchen counter. "So, what's going on with the murder investigation?"

"It's frustrating. We know Cooper had been conning older women and getting enough money to live large, but, so far, that doesn't really point to a motive for murder."

"But, Cooper was in his fifties. He didn't just start conning people a year ago. I'm sure he had a colorful past."

"And, my love, we are checking it out very carefully. No worries. Oh, guess who I ran into the other day: Ellen Green."

"Wow! She and Charlie are back? And, what perfect timing! Maybe they'll solve this murder, too," Jennifer teased.

Raul grimaced but said absolutely nothing.

41

Saturday, March 2

Ellen and Charlie were sitting on the lanai. They had just finished the almond croissants that they had bought at the Farmers' Market. Ellen was still savoring her second mug of coffee when Charlie announced that he planned to spend the afternoon on the dock with his paints and easel.

"Sounds good. I think I'll take a bike ride," Ellen stated, getting up to clear the table. She was eager to see Beverly Miller and didn't want Charlie to know about it. Beverly might, unwittingly, be able to provide a detail or description that could prove useful. Ellen got on a bike and quickly peddled to Miramar Court.

Beverly answered the door and invited Ellen inside. "You're lucky. You caught me on my day off."

"Your day off?" Ellen asked.

"Yes. Saturday is the one day I don't play tennis."

"Oh, I see. Well, I was just taking a bike ride and thought I'd stop in and say 'hello'."

"You might as well stay for coffee. I only have decaf," Beverly offered, less than graciously.

"Thanks. I'd love some," Ellen smiled, silently cringing.

Beverly returned with two mugs of decaf and joined Ellen on the lanai. Ellen knew better than to bother with small talk. She and Beverly, both, preferred the direct, in-your-face approach to conversations. "So, Beverly, about Cooper."

"What about him?"

"Well, you were with him the night before he was killed. Did he give any hint about being worried for his safety?"

"Ellen, this was our first date. I certainly wasn't looking to be his therapist or his mother!"

Ellen was summarily shut down, but that didn't stop her. "It seems that lots of women donated generously to his music studio fund. Did he try to get you to donate?"

"If I made a donation, I would have done it by choice. I don't succumb to pressure," Beverly answered impatiently.

"Did you contribute to his fund?"

"If I did, it's no concern of yours. Besides, it turns out that there was no music studio fund. Cooper was bilking us all," she uttered with venom.

"What? There was no music studio fund?" Ellen was shocked to hear this. "What makes you say that?"

"The young detective who showed up the day after the murder told me. He said that Cooper had conned a lot of women out of a lot of money."

"But why did the detective tell you about that?"

Beverly adopted an imperious tone as she explained, "During my dinner with Cooper, he talked passionately about his vision for the music studio. So, I agreed to make a small donation that evening. Not nearly as much as Cooper had asked me for. And, apparently, much smaller than most of his donors make, mind you. And, I wrote him a check. I never make a donation in cash."

"So, the detective came to tell you that there was no music studio fund?"

"That, and, to say that my check was found in Cooper's pocket when he was, um, when he was found --dead."

Detective Raul Swann was waiting at police headquarters. He had hoped to spend the day at the beach with Jennifer but, first, he had a short list of interviews to conduct regarding the Cooper murder. Fortunately, his first interview arrived right on time: Dr. Paul Shapiro.

"Dr. Shapiro, I'm Detective Sergeant Raul Swann. Thanks for coming in today." Raul leaned across his desk to shake hands. He gestured to the chair facing him.

"Detective." Shapiro nodded. "You realize you made me give up my golf game for today," he winked.

Raul got straight to the business at hand. "Dr. Shapiro, your name was listed on Cooper's mobile phone. The department is routinely

44

interviewing every contact. Please describe your relationship to the deceased."

"Sure. He was one of my patients."

"And, when did you first meet Cooper?"

"Hmm, he came to see me about a year ago. He had recently moved to Cape Coral."

"Did you get to know Cooper?"

"Well, Detective, I got to know his teeth very well. He came in every couple of months for a cleaning."

"Did you know him personally?"

"Cooper was strictly a patient. If you mean were we friends, I'd have to say no. But I guess you could say we were acquaintances. A couple of times, I met up with him for drinks at the Boat House."

"What was Cooper like?"

"Very friendly. He seemed like an easy-going guy. But, as a patient, I barely saw him. The hygienist did the cleaning. I just came in and checked his teeth. Oh, but the receptionists loved it when he came in! He let them take photos on their phones with him--that sort of thing," Shapiro smiled.

"Did you donate any money to his senior music studio fund?"

"Now, why would I do that?"

"Please, answer the question. Did you donate money to his senior music studio fund?"

"No. If I contributed to every organization that hit me up for a donation, I'd be on food stamps by now!"

"Dr. Shapiro, we're looking for any information that could help us find his killer," Raul sighed. "Is there anyone or anything you can tell me that might help?"

Paul Shapiro thought for a moment before replying. "I wish I could help you, Detective. But, if I think of anything, I'll contact you. Do you have a card?"

Raul handed Dr. Shapiro a business card and thanked him. Then, Raul took a few minutes to prepare for the next interview awaiting him.

That evening, Charlie was in very good spirits as he poured two glasses of wine. It had been the kind of Cape Coral day he loved. His painting of the boats docked all along the length of the canal was beginning to take shape. Later, he and Ellen watched the sun set from the Boat House and returned home to fix a pasta salad for dinner.

As Charlie walked onto the lanai, he could see the hot tub lights changing color every two seconds. Ellen was already submerged, waiting for him. "Here, Ellen. Hold onto these," he said passing both glasses to her.

"Let's toast to a wonderful day." They clinked glasses and took a sip.

"Charlie, what if Cooper never really had a legitimate music studio fund," she blurted out.

"Ellen, what are you talking about?" he asked. Without waiting for a response, he continued, "Why don't you just tell me what you were really up to this afternoon." He sighed, took a long drink, and braced himself for the inevitable.

Monday, March 4

"Good morning, officers," Captain McConnell greeted the department. "We have updates and want to brief all of you on the status of the Cooper murder investigation. Detective Swann will take over from here."

"Thank-you, Captain. New information regarding the murder victim has been discovered. As you already know, Cooper, A.K.A. Mark Simmons, moved to Cape Coral in February 2018, one year ago. His address is listed as 1324 Jackson Lane. However, his real home was his penthouse apartment at 750 Crimson Court. During his tenure here, Cooper bankrolled over one million dollars from donations to his bogus music studio fund. The contributions were, primarily, in cash from ladies who could very well be your mothers and grandmothers." Raul paused to let this sink in, scanning the room of officers facing him.

"Over the weekend our tech team made a significant breakthrough." Raul pressed a key on his laptop to project a photo onto the large screen behind him. It was a grainy, black and white photo of a young man. "Now, if I split the screen and show you this second photo, you'll see the resemblance." The room full of seasoned, professional police officers and detectives viewed a photo of Cooper, on the right, and a photo of Cooper thirty years prior, on the left. Raul continued. "Mark Simmons, on your left, was a truck driver back in the late 80's. Our sources say that he smuggled drugs from the Mexican border in Juarez to New Orleans. Now, nobody seems to know exactly what Mark Simmons' role was. He may have had no idea what he was carrying in the back of that truck. But, we do know that back in

48

1989, his truck was found abandoned outside of El Paso. Mark disappeared. Yes, officer?"

"Sir, that was thirty years ago. Any info on his whereabouts since then?"

"The team is checking that out now. We'll know more very soon. Thanks, officers, for your diligence and dedication. Remember: be safe, be smart, and be thorough." Raul stepped down and Captain McConnell adjourned the meeting.

Pizza night at Maria's was always lively, but tonight the restaurant was abuzz about a news story. And surprisingly, the lead article that appeared in the Fort Myers News-Press had nothing to do with the Cooper murder. A vicious act had rocked the community: a man had destroyed a burrowing owl nest that was located in an underground pipe smack in the middle of his construction site.

"Of course, he deserved to be arrested!" Catherine proclaimed.

Karen added, "I agree. He's lucky he wasn't charged with murder!"

"Now, just a minute. He violated a city ordinance, but I think that a steep fine would have sent a clear message," Bud said calmly.

Ted concurred but with reservations. "Maybe, but this guy destroyed one of Cape Coral's greatest wonders of nature. Do you realize that there is a heavier concentration of burrowing owls in Cape Coral than anywhere else in Florida?"

"The burrowing owls are an endangered species," Karen pointed out. "And now, one generation of babies has been eliminated!"

"Look, give the guy a break," Bud argued. "Okay, he was supposed to wait another five months until the babies left the nest before starting construction. But, face it, he probably thought his business might not survive the delay."

"Bud, he should have thought, period. Hah! You think his business will survive his jail term?" Catherine retorted.

Charlie tried to diffuse the tension. "Protecting the burrowing owls seems to be the one and only issue that even the local politicians agree upon. So, why the hell are all of us arguing about it?"

"Arguing? Whooo?" Bud quipped with a smile and a shrug.

Tuesday, March 5

"Ellen, open up!" Catherine yelled, knocking on the door.

Charlie got to the door first. "Catherine, come on in. You okay?"

"Of course, I'm okay. I need to show something to Ellen. Where is she?"

"She's just getting out of the shower."

"Well, tell her to hurry up. I don't have much time."

"I'll get her. But, how about some coffee?"

"Sure. A little--and I mean a little-- milk and no sugar, please."

Charlie summoned Ellen and she greeted Catherine just as the coffee was ready. "Catherine, what's up?"

"Thought you might be interested in this obituary dated February 10, 2019. I decided to do a little research." She read aloud from the Breeze. *"Mildred Smith Blake, of Mangrove Court, passed away on February 8, 2019 at age 92 of natural causes. She is survived by her loving son, Frank Blake, of Cape Coral. Mildred was born in Cleveland, Ohio and had lived there until she moved to Cape Coral, twenty-eight years ago.*

Mildred was an active member of the Yacht Club Senior Center. She rarely missed a bingo night and always enjoyed line dancing and tai chi classes. In the last year, Mildred developed a fondness for music. She became a devoted fan of the singer/guitar player, Cooper.

51

Private arrangements are being made for her cremation. In lieu of flowers, friends and family have requested that donations be made to the Cooper Senior Music Studio Fund."

Looking directly at Ellen, Catherine said, "Now, you need to tell me what's going on."

Charlie quickly intercepted the statement. "Catherine, nothing is going on. Right, Ellen?"

At that instant, Ellen had the misfortune of biting down much too hard on an almond biscotti. "My tooth!" she cried out. "I think I just chipped my tooth!"

"Don't worry. I can give you the name of my dentist. You'll be fine. But, now, tell me what's going on," Catherine eyed both of them suspiciously.

"Nothing," they said in unison.

Catherine folded her arms across her chest and looked amused. "Come on, Ellen. I know this has to do with the Cooper murder."

Ellen caved and proceeded to tell Catherine about Beverly Miller and about Mildred's will. "And, what can I say? I admit, I'm curious. Cooper was, definitely, a con artist. But, at the same time, he made a lot of women feel really valued. Why would someone want to murder him?"

"Plenty of reasons," Catherine replied. "Every celebrity risks their life. You can be sure that there's always a nutcase out there ready to kill a celebrity--even if he's a second-rate, small-town nobody." With that comment, Catherine left the obituary on the counter, wrote down the name of her dentist, and said good-bye.

"Well, at least, now I know what I have to do today," Ellen said with certainty.

"I'm afraid, that's pretty obvious," Charlie commiserated.

"Can you help me find his number on the computer?"

"Of course, Sweetie. What's his name?"

"Frank, Frank Blake. And, Charlie, thanks," Ellen said, somewhat surprised by Charlie's acquiescence.

"What? Frank Blake? Ellen, I'm talking about making an appointment with the dentist. You just chipped your tooth!"

Dr. Paul Shapiro's office was able to fit Ellen in for an appointment on Thursday. Fortunately, she was not in any pain. In the meantime, Ellen was on her laptop, in hot pursuit of Frank Blake's address. Her phone "can-canned". She answered it, "Pamela!"

"Hi, Ellen. Wondered if you were back in Cape Coral yet."

"Yes, we got here just over a week ago. How are you and Ron?"

"We're doing well. We just returned from Tuscany last week. How's Charlie?"

"As unmanageable as ever!"

53

"And, you wouldn't want it any other way, would you? Listen, I'm calling to invite you, both, to a sunset cocktail party this Friday. I know it's short notice."

"Pamela, we wouldn't miss it! Thanks so much."

"Wonderful. Come to the terrace at Marker 92 around 5:00."

"Great! Looking forward to seeing you and Ron. Bye, Pamela."

"See you Friday, Ellen."

Ron and Pamela Green are the owners of the luxurious Cape Coral Resort at Marina Village. The Greens had all met a year ago when Charlie discovered that he and Ron, not only, shared the same last name but shared a penchant for over-the-top gestures. Ron and Pamela played a pivotal role in helping to solve the murder on the Caloosahatchee.

Ellen decided that locating Frank Blake would, simply, have to wait. Pamela's invitation had precipitated a wardrobe emergency. She, certainly, could not show up at Ron and Pamela's party in the same outfit she wore last year. A trip to Miromar Outlets was in order this afternoon.

Ellen told Charlie about the call from Pamela and explained that Pamela's invitation required a shopping trip. Charlie could care less about her explanation. He was delighted by her news and relieved that Ellen seemed to have forgotten about this Frank Blake guy. In fact, now he was free to play golf.

"Ellen, could you drop me off at Sunset Bay Golf Course on your way? I'm going to try to get in a quick round. I'm sure I can get a ride home from someone later."

"No problem! Can you be ready in ten minutes?"

"Of course."

Sunset Bay Golf Course was busy when Ellen dropped Charlie off. He checked in at the pro shop and it wasn't long before he was asked to join a threesome about to tee off: Mike, Stan, and Paul. They welcomed Charlie into their group, despite his being a snowbird. After a genial round of golf, they all headed to the bar for a couple of beers, grabbing the last four seats.

"So, what do you make of the Cooper murder?" Mike asked.

"Probably some pissed off husband killed him," answered Stan, taking a drink of his beer.

"Yeah. Can't say I'm sorry the guy is dead. My wife thinks flags should be lowered to half mast, she's so upset," Mike said. "Paul, you're lucky that your girlfriend isn't old enough to be one of his groupies!"

"Can't say that any more, guys," Paul remarked glibly. "We broke up a few weeks ago. It was mutual. No big deal."

"Well, this Cooper guy sure had a good thing going! Women couldn't wait to give him money and all he had to do was show up and do a couple of these." The rather blubbery man next to Charlie stood up and attempted a few Elvis pelvis thrusts. Guffaws were heard all the way to the first tee.

"I think the guy was scamming those women. Probably just pocketed the money for himself. That's what I think," another golfer commented, at the far end of the bar.

"Well Frank, who's part of our foursome, had nothing good to say about Cooper." Paul explained, "Frank's mother died and left her entire estate to this Cooper guy!"

"She must have been out of her friggin' mind to do that!" one of the golfers said. "Who is this guy Frank?"

"Frank. Frank Blake. You've probably seen him here with us before. Kind of a hefty guy."

Charlie had been drinking his beer and minding his own business, but, hearing the name "Frank Blake" sucked him right in. "Hey, Tom, how about another round for my foursome--on me."

"Sure. Here you go, guys. Drink up!" Tom, the bartender said, placing a Stella if front of each of them.

"So, did Frank contest the will or anything?" Charlie threw into the conversation.

"I don't know," Paul said. "But, it's a shame. Frank didn't deserve that. And, he was really pissed, I have to say."

Another guy chimed in, "I don't blame him!"

"Hey, I better get going. I'm already late," Paul said, checking his watch. "Got an emergency root canal waiting! Anybody live near Frank? I found his pitching wedge in my bag and promised to return it to him."

Stan offered to drop off the club. "Stan, thanks! That helps me out. I'll leave his club next to your bag. Gotta run! See ya'!"

"Where does Frank live?" Charlie asked.

"S.W. El Dorado Parkway."

"That's not far from me. Would you mind taking me home to Wisteria Court?" Charlie asked.

"No problem, Charlie," Stan replied.

Mike said, finishing his beer, "Ya know, it's funny, but about a year ago we had another murder in Cape Coral."

Charlie coolly mused, "Hmm. I vaguely remember that. That is a strange coincidence. Here we are just one year later." He shook his head thoughtfully.

"Yeah. Strange coincidence. Who'd have thunk it. Right here in Cape Coral," Stan muttered. "Oh well, Charlie, you ready to go?"

Ellen's afternoon had been a series of frustrations. Her goal was to shop for an outfit that looked like she hadn't shopped for an outfit. However, at seventy-one, Ellen discovered that anything clingy showed bulges that, she could swear, weren't there the day before. And, anything loose and flowy made her look like a tent on toothpicks.

When she returned home, she decided, instead, to focus on locating Frank Blake. After hours of researching, she uncovered a twenty-two-year-old Frank Blake, a Frank Blake who died at the ripe old age of ninety-seven, and an eighty-year-old Frank Joseph Blake who was arrested for exposing himself at the public beach.

By hot tub time, Ellen was feeling dumpy and discouraged. Therefore, Charlie's cheerfulness served only to annoy her further. "You must have had one hell of a golf game today," Ellen grumbled.

"It was okay. The starter teamed me up with a nice threesome. Hope I get to play with them again."

"Well, my afternoon sucked. I feel fat and frumpy and frustrated."

Charlie shifted his body to her side of the tub and edged close to her. "Sweetie, you're beautiful to me. You know that, don't you?"

Ellen leaned into Charlie's shoulder. "Thanks, Charlie."

"Besides," Charlie continued, "I happen to know where we can find a certain Frank Blake."

"What?" Ellen was stunned. "I wasted my entire day looking for his address! You go to play golf, have a couple of beers, and you find him? Just like that?"

Charlie winked. "Yup." In spite of herself, Ellen couldn't help but be ecstatic about this news. She threw her arms around his neck.

"Shit," he thought to himself. "What the hell have I done?" He knew he couldn't un-ring the bell.

Wednesday, March 6

Early this morning, Captain McConnell and Detective Swann were meeting privately. Detective Swann was providing an update on the status of the Cooper investigation. He explained that they are working in cooperation with investigators from El Paso to New Orleans. "We, now, have confirmed that Cooper, A.K.A. Mark Simmons, was a mule. Twice per week he picked up a shipment from El Paso and drove it to New Orleans. Cooper drove the same route from 1985 to 1989. He was smuggling drugs, just as we had suspected."

"Do we know who he worked for?"

"No, Captain. But, we do know that Cooper had no idea what he was transporting and, probably, didn't want to know. Then, in November 1989, it appears that he decided to find out. He abandoned his truck outside of El Paso and disappeared."

"Who are these sources, Swann?"

"Captain, our out-of-state partners would never reveal their sources. You know that. But, they confirm that the sources are credible."

"Okay. Go on."

"Now here's where it gets interesting. For the next thirty years, Mark Simmons became Justin Cooper: waiter, handyman, house painter, you name it. He never stayed anywhere more than a year or two. Must have been on the run from his contacts back when he was smuggling drugs."

60

"So, where did he live between '89 and 2018?"

"All over the country. He was in California. Settled in La Jolla and Santa Rosa for a few years. Then, he went to some small town in Montana for eighteen months. Spent time in New Mexico. Moved to Austin, Peoria, Illinois, then to Chicago. Lived in Atlanta, Bowling Green, Kentucky, and even moved to Harrisburg, PA. No police record. He was clean. Kept to himself and never had any significant relationships."

Captain McConnell was about to ask a question when they heard shouting from outside the building. They both raced to look out the window. "What the fuck is going on out there?" Captain McConnell yelled to no one in particular.

Hundreds of women, mostly well past their prime, had assembled on the steps and sidewalk in front of the Cape Coral Police Department. They were chanting, "WHO KILLED COOPER? WE DEMAND TO KNOW. FIND HIS KILLER OR WATCH OUR ANGER GROW!" Placards with "AGE IS NOT A NUMBER" and poster-size photos of Cooper blocked the entire street.

McConnell made an announcement to all the officers in the building. "Get the hell outside. Shut them up and move them out. Stat!"

"Sir," Raul said cautiously, "is that really the best approach? They have a right to assemble peacefully."

"You call that peaceful?" McConnell growled.

"Well, Sir, yes, I do. Maybe it wouldn't be a bad idea to offer to meet with the organizers of this group."

"Swann, tell me honestly," he said pointing from the window to the angry mob below, "would you want to meet with any of them? Huh?"

Before Raul could respond, they both saw a couple of reporters and the WINK TV cameras getting it all on film.

McConnell and Swann bolted down the stairs to gather the officers before any over-zealous cop started spraying tear gas into the crowd. "Officers, get in here ASAP!" McConnell ordered, gesturing to the meeting room near the lobby.

Seeing the press show up had an immediate impact on McConnell's demeanor. "Okay, listen up. Here's what we're going to do. Officers Bradley and O'Riley get out there to redirect the street traffic. Murray, Gilroy, and Patterson establish a perimeter and be polite to these broads." McConnell shook his finger at the officers. "Remember to smile and be courteous. This will end up on page one tomorrow!"

As McConnell adjourned the crisis meeting, he growled to Raul, "And, you, Swann, get out there and talk to the reporters."

"But, sir..."

"Now!"

Raul took a deep breath and opened the front door. As he scanned the angry mob, he would have preferred to be facing down a full-blown prison riot rather than this group. Before he had a chance to say anything, reporters from the Fort Myers News-Press and the Cape Coral Daily Breeze were shouting questions at him. "Have the police made progress in the Cooper investigation?" "Do you have a possible suspect?" "Is the murderer someone local?" "What do you make of the protest?"

Raul spoke in his most professional and respectful tone. "Good morning. Although this protest comes as a surprise, these women are assembling peacefully and are exercising their rights as Americans." At that moment, several of the protesters got in Raul's face and started screaming, "Find Cooper's killer. Find Cooper's killer! Find him now!"

"Sir, please answer my question," yelled one of the reporters over the noise of the crowd.

"Certainly," he smiled as the cameras from WINK TV started rolling. "The department has made excellent progress. At this time, we do not have a suspect, but we are working around the clock to follow every, single lead. We have expanded our investigation and are working in cooperation with law enforcement from other states. I would like to send this message to Cooper's killer. If you're watching this, know that we are closing in and will find you!" Raul warned.

The protesters were starting to swarm around Raul. "We demand action!"

Raul remained composed. "I know you are all devoted fans who are, understandably, upset. Captain McConnell and I would like to meet with you to hear your frustrations and concerns. Who are the organizers of this protest?"

Two rather imposing women stepped forward. "We are," one of them proclaimed.

Raul, immediately, radioed Captain McConnell and informed him that he was heading inside so they could meet with two of the organizers. He flashed his disarmingly boyish smile. "Please, ladies, come with me."

A few minutes later, the organizers emerged from the meeting, visibly shaken by what they had learned. "Ladies, ladies!" one of the leaders shouted into the microphone. She stopped and waited as the crowd settled down. All eyes were fixed on the two women.

"We have just met with the officers overseeing the murder investigation. It seems that our beloved Cooper never had a Senior Music Studio Fund. In other words, he stole our money. It was all a scam." This shocking announcement was met with a collective gasp. Everyone seemed to be frozen in place.

All at once, an inexplicable transformation occurred. From the very back of the crowd, a few voices began singing Cooper's signature song: the Beatles' "Michelle". The voices grew louder as more women joined in. Soon, the angry mob became a united front. They all held hands and poured their hearts out, as one.

Much to Charlie's relief, Ellen hadn't mentioned anything more about finding Frank Blake. In fact, he and Ellen were looking forward to spending several hours at the Six-Mile Cypress Slough in nearby Fort Myers. This nature preserve is a beautifully maintained, forested wetland. The cypress slough acts as a filter for water flowing through on its way to Estero Bay. Ellen and Charlie visited here every year to stroll the one-mile loop, meandering along the boardwalk and carefully following the annotated brochure. They thoroughly enjoyed this opportunity to walk slowly and quietly. They remembered to look up, stand very still, and actively listen. At times, they both closed their eyes and were aware of sounds that had been overshadowed by visual stimulation.

However, dinner that evening was in total contrast to their peaceful afternoon. Ellen and Charlie headed to Slate's, in Cape Coral, for dinner at the bar. This taste of New Orleans had become a favorite of theirs. The chef-owners, Allan and Nancy Cotter, had previously owned the critically acclaimed Blue Moon Restaurant and Jazz Club on St. Croix for sixteen years. In 2010, they had every intention of moving to Cape Coral to just kick back and retire but, instead, opened up Slate's--much to the delight of the Cape Coral/Fort Myers community.

It wasn't long before, Bob, the bartender's rich baritone voice greeted Ellen and Charlie. "Welcome back, you, two!"

"Thanks. Great to be here, Bob," Charlie said. "How have you been?"

"Chugging along just fine, Charlie. The usual? And for you, Ellen?" Bob asked while mixing a Hurricane and an Espresso Martini for the couple seated on Charlie's left.

Ellen and Charlie were enjoying their drinks. "Bob, when you get a chance, could you order me half a dozen raw oysters?"

Bob nodded, "Coming right up, Charlie!"

A few minutes later, they placed their dinner orders. Ellen began chatting with the young woman seated next to her. Maya, a transplant from Cleveland, had been living in Cape Coral since last April. She was a slender woman in her late forties with a shiny, jet black bob and penetrating, brown eyes. Her pale, wrinkle-free complexion defied the Florida sun. Maya and Ellen were both raving about Hot Buttered Nuggets, the husband-wife duo performing at Slate's Sidedoor Jazz Club, when the entrees arrived.

The aroma, alone, of Ellen's boneless short ribs distracted her from the conversation, momentarily. Maya continued, "I get to hear the best music because I free-lance as a sound-tech for many musicians in the Fort Myers/Cape Coral area."

"Really?" Ellen mumbled, her mouth full with an explosion of flavors.

"Yup. I always loved music and, now, I get to help create the sounds."

Charlie was too busy digging into his pan-seared scallops to pay any attention to Ellen's conversation. "That must get pretty complex," Ellen said, elbowing Charlie. "Oh, Maya, I'd like you to meet my husband, Charlie."

Charlie turned and shook hands with Maya, giving her his most courtly nod. "Pleased to meet you, Maya."

Maya smiled in return. "Anyway, I keep away from the complicated stuff, but I can make the acoustic players project a more balanced sound, especially when they perform outside," Maya replied, taking a generous drink of her beer.

"Did you ever work for Cooper?" Ellen asked.

Maya shrugged her shoulders in a show of indifference. "Yeah, a number of times."

"What was he like to work for?"

"He was very, uh, focused. He always knew what he wanted to do and knew just how to get the job done."

"Sounds like you knew him pretty well."

"You could say that," Maya smiled wistfully. "Actually, I really didn't know him well. We had worked closely together. But, that was the extent of our relationship."

"How are you dealing with his murder?" Ellen asked, plunging right into the heart of the issue.

"I'm okay." She took the last swig of her beer, swiveled her stool around, and turned to Ellen. "Nice to have met you, Ellen. You too, Charlie."

Ellen smiled, "I enjoyed meeting you, too, Maya. Hope to see you here again."

Charlie waved, "Same here."

Thursday, March 7

This morning was sunny and crisp. It was, indeed, promising to be a perfect spring day in Cape Coral. Charlie walked to the beach, belting out Billy Joel's "Piano Man" completely out of tune. He was anticipating a fantastic morning all by himself. He planned to do some sketching on the beach and read a little, sitting at his favorite picnic table, shaded by lush palm trees.

When he arrived at the beach, he strode out onto the pier hoping to catch a sighting of Ellen as she finished up her run. Charlie still got a bit of a rush when he saw her approaching. He never understood how Ellen could manage to run like a gazelle but trip walking down the sidewalk.

They walked into the Boat House as Jay, the manager, came over to shake hands. "Hey, welcome back, Ellen and Charlie!"

"Great to be here, Jay," Charlie replied.

"Hi, Jay. What a crowd this morning! What's going on? You giving away free Bloody Marys?" Ellen asked. Jay shrugged his shoulders, shook his head, and hustled over to help one of the servers.

Charlie's attempts to order a couple of coffees were futile in the midst of excessive noise. Above the racket, they could barely catch snippets. Finally, Amy found them and came over with their coffees.

"Amy, what's going on today?" Ellen asked.

"You haven't heard? Well, hundreds of women protested outside of the police station yesterday." Amy summed up the lead article in the

68

Breeze. "And, now, everyone knows that the Senior Music Studio Fund was nothing but a scam!"

Reactions at the Boat House were divided entirely along gender lines. "Hah, I knew the guy was a con artist," one guy commented.

"Yeah. Sure was! My wife better not have given the bastard any money," retorted another.

"Well, you know what, Henry, I'd be happy to give you money if you talked to me the way Cooper talked," Henry's wife shot back.

Another woman piped up, "I agree. For the first time since that age between acne and pregnancy, I actually felt beautiful."

The jousting continued, gaining momentum, when, reluctantly, Ellen realized it was time for her to head to the dentist's office.

Ellen arrived at 2700 Del Prado Boulevard for her appointment with Dr. Paul Shapiro. She found herself in a modern suite of offices with floor to ceiling tinted windows in the waiting area. The receptionist who greeted her had a fake British accent, but Ellen didn't care. Even a fake British accent conveyed class and efficiency. She gave her name and, as soon as she heard the name "Cooper" mentioned, strained to overhear the two other receptionists. They were buzzing about Cooper's murder in hushed tones. Ellen couldn't make out a single word.

Within a reasonable time, Ellen was escorted to room 3B where she met with the hygienist to describe her complaint. Dr. Shapiro arrived and introduced himself. He was in his mid-fifties, trim, and of average height. His deliberate five o'clock shadow gave him a sexy appearance--a far cry from the pasty-faced dentist back home.

"Mrs. Green," he smiled shaking her hand, "I'm Dr. Paul Shapiro. Are you in any pain?"

"Pleased to meet you, Dr. Shapiro. No, no pain at all."

"Well, let's have a look," he said, almost playfully. "Aha, there is that nasty little chipped tooth. I'm going to have Darlene take some x-rays, I'll check them over, and we'll see what we need to do."

Ellen was quite content to spend the morning with Dr. Shapiro, if need be. She wanted to be sure to thank Catherine for her excellent taste in dentists. After Darlene took the x-rays, Ellen waited patiently for Dr. Shapiro to return, wishing she had worn her swishy, tie-dyed skirt instead of her boot-cut jeans. She checked out the decor. A grouping of three framed watercolors were directly across from her. Each painting depicted a different wildflower. On the wall to her right, was the obligatory chart showing various stages of progressive gum disease. To her left was a collage of black and white photos of bridges: suspension, pedestrian, and covered. Ellen chuckled to herself at the double meaning. She was quite sure that this was intentional.

Dr. Shapiro returned and summed up the situation. Ellen would need two more appointments to properly prepare a mold, fit, and secure a crown. He told her to check with his receptionist regarding insurance coverage before scheduling the next appointment.

70

Ellen stopped by the desk and saw that the receptionists still seemed to be gossiping, but loudly enough for Ellen to hear them without appearing to eavesdrop. She interjected, "You heard the latest about Cooper, I take it?" They nodded.

The one receptionist answered, "We almost feel as if we knew him. He was a patient of Dr. Shapiro and he was always so friendly and," she blushed, "really cute, too! We can't believe he scammed everyone. It doesn't seem possible."

"I'm so sorry," Ellen said.

In the meantime, Charlie had set up his easel next to the picnic table. He gazed out and saw that the beach was sprinkled with families staking out their turf, a leathery-skinned woman doing tai chi, and elderly men stooped over their metal detectors. As Charlie began to sketch, he attracted a few curious vacationers. They assumed that he was a local artist and asked if they could take selfies with him to send to their friends in the middle of an Arctic blast back in Minneapolis.

After a couple of hours, Charlie decided to stretch his legs. He got up and walked down the length of the pier overlooking the Caloosahatchee. Charlie splayed his arms out and placed his hands on the rail, admiring the beauty, the calm, and the vibrant colors spread out before him.

"Hey, is that you, Charlie?" asked a familiar voice behind him.

Charlie turned around and was greeted by Bud. "Bud, nice surprise!"

"Well, so, this is the very spot where it all began," Bud said, remembering the murder of Jack Newman, one year ago.

Charlie nodded in agreement. "What are you doing down here?"

"Just finished playing racquetball."

"Hey, do you have time for some coffee?"

"Sure, Charlie." They both walked back to the Boat House and sat at the bar.

"Bud, hi. Mind if I join you guys?"

"Of course not. Eli Thompson, Charlie Green. Eli just joined the racquetball league," Bud explained.

"Nice to meet you, Eli."

"So, how do you know Bud?" Eli asked.

"Through my sister-in-law, Catherine. My wife, Ellen, and I are snowbirds. We rent a house on Wisteria Court every winter."

"Nice location. Welcome to Cape Coral," Eli nodded to Charlie and they shook hands. They all looked up at the large TV screen in the back of the bar. WINK, a CBS affiliate, was rebroadcasting their entire footage of yesterday's protest. Charlie was stunned by the fervor of the women. Eli was more than stunned. He was furious. "Look at those stupid broads! The guy screws them over, steals their money, and they still think he's the greatest thing since Elvis."

"I don't get it either," agreed Bud.

72

"Well, maybe we can learn a thing or two from Cooper," Charlie joshed.

"Let me tell you something, Charlie," Eli warned, shaking his finger at him as he spoke. "That bastard was like a disease."

"What are you talking about?"

"Cooper was all my wife talked about for the last six months or so. He deserved what he got!"

At hot tub time, Ellen and Charlie, good-naturedly, rehashed the protest and the Boat House battle of the sexes. Ellen loved that the women had been emboldened by Cooper. A revolution led by a mob of post-menopausal women! Charlie didn't bother to remind Ellen that Cooper had stolen their money. He knew there was no point in attempting to reason with Ellen once her feminist DNA kicked into gear.

Instead, he asked, "Ellen, by the way, how was the dentist appointment? You haven't said a thing about it."

"Actually, Charlie, it wasn't bad at all. Dr. Paul Shapiro seems like a good dentist and a nice guy."

"Paul, you said?"

"Yes, that's his name. Why?"

"I played golf with a Paul who's a dentist. Could be the same guy."

73

"In his fifties, dark stubble, kinda sexy?" Ellen inquired mischievously.

"In answer to your questions: yes, yes, and, no, I didn't find him kinda sexy. But, Ellen, my favorite feminist, isn't that a rather sexist comment to make about your dentist?" Charlie teased, "I may have to report you to the gender police."

"Alright, Charlie. Touché!"

Ellen settled down and enjoyed the rush of warm water on her back. Charlie was the first to break the silence, for a change. "Well, today I learned that Cooper may have had his female fans, but he sure made some enemies!"

Ellen's eyes remained closed, so Charlie continued. "I met this guy, Eli, today. His wife was gaga over Cooper and Eli said that Cooper deserved to be killed."

That got Ellen's attention in a hurry. "You're serious?"

"That's what he said. And, he was one pissed-off husband!"

"Well, now we know of two guys who hated his guts."

"Two?" Charlie asked, confused.

"Mildred Blake's son, Frank. You remember. He got screwed out of his inheritance. And, tomorrow I intend to find out exactly how much Frank Blake hated Cooper!"

"Oh, really, Ellen? And, how do you plan to do that?"

"It's very simple. You told me you left his golf club next to his front door so, obviously, you know where Frank Blake lives," Ellen smiled with glee.

Charlie regretted telling Ellen about that, but it was too late. "And, just what do you intend to say to Frank Blake, Ellen?"

Ellen thought for a moment before replying. "I'm not going to say anything. You're going to do all the talking, Charlie."

Friday, March 8

For the entire drive to S.W. El Dorado Parkway, Charlie grumbled about this morning's outing. Ellen knew better than to try to cajole him out of his mood. The fact that he was there with her and would do all the talking was enough to satisfy Ellen. As they slowly approached Frank's house, the homes on this street became very modest, but tidy. "Okay, Ellen, Frank Blake lives right here."

They went to the front door and rang the bell. Charlie hoped that no one would answer. However, that was not the case. A stocky man in his sixties came to the door. He was wearing shorts, a tee shirt, and flip-flops.

"Yes?" he asked.

"Hi, I'm Charlie Green and this is my wife, Ellen. We're looking for a Frank Blake."

"What do you want with Frank?"

Before Charlie could respond, Ellen, who suddenly seemed to forget that she had not wanted to say anything, blurted out, "We wanted to pay our respects. You see, I knew his mother, Mildred."

"I'm Frank. Please come on in." They entered a very small, simple home that probably looked the same as it did back in the '70's. Frank invited them to sit down on the brown, Naugahyde couch. "How did you know my mother?"

Charlie decided to kick back, play it cool, and watch Ellen get herself tangled in her web of lies. "Well," she began, "Frank, could I please have a glass of water?"

Frank went into the kitchen. Charlie whispered, "a glass of water?"

"I need time to come up with a story," Ellen snapped impatiently.

"Here you are," Frank said, handing her a glass.

"Thank-you, Frank," she smiled.

"So, tell me, how did you know my mother?"

"We met at a Cooper concert." Ellen watched closely. Was it her imagination or did Frank grimace at the mention of Cooper? Ellen said, "Your mother was a great fan of his, you know."

When Frank did not respond, Ellen continued, "My friend Stella often drove your mother to his concerts. That's how we met. Cooper made your mother very happy, Frank."

"Hah! Cooper scammed everyone. You must have read about it in yesterday's paper," Frank said vehemently.

"But, Frank," Ellen leaned towards him, tilting her head slightly. She spoke gently, "your mother wouldn't have cared. Cooper made her feel beautiful and special. In fact, she thought of Cooper as a, well," Ellen sighed before finishing her sentence, "almost as a second son."

Frank, abruptly, stood up and began rubbing his hands together angrily. "How can you say that! I've had it with this Cooper. He took advantage of elderly women and, you know what? I'm glad he's dead!"

Before Ellen could provoke Frank any further, Charlie stepped in. "Frank, we'll leave, now." He took Ellen's arm to hurry her out the door.

"Your mother was a lovely woman," Ellen craned her neck and yelled to Frank as the door slammed in her face.

The Cape Coral Police Department had scheduled an entire day of interviews. They pulled in every contact of Cooper's they could locate. This morning, Maya Wolfson was nervously awaiting questioning. Detective Sergeant Raul Swann met her in the waiting area and escorted her to his office.

"Please have a seat, Ms. Wolfson," he said, gesturing to a chair facing his desk. "You do understand that the department is questioning every known contact of Cooper's. Would you, please, verify your name and address for me?"

"Maya Wolfson, 436 Santa Barbara Boulevard, Cape Coral."

"Thank-you. How long have you lived in Cape Coral, Ms. Wolfson?"

"I moved here last April-- April 2018, less than a year ago."

"Where were you living before?"

"I moved from Cleveland. I was working as a sound-tech for a few local groups. Did some radio work, even filled in as a back-up singer here and there," she said modestly.

"Why did you move here?"

"Detective, do you remember the winter of 2018? I'll bet you don't!" Maya laughed. "Well, that alone would've convinced me to head South, but then I heard a Cooper concert." Raul waited for Maya to continue. "I got a good deal on a flight to Fort Myers back in February. It was just for a long weekend, but I heard Cooper at the Fort Myers Flea Market. It was one of his first gigs. He charmed the crowd, but he didn't have any idea how to project at a venue like that."

"Go on."

"I waited until he finished and introduced myself. I told him what he needed to do to improve the sound quality. He invited me for a drink so we could talk some more. Before we finished, I offered to come to Cape Coral and work for him."

"Just like that? You picked up and moved?" Raul asked somewhat surprised.

"Yeah, why not?" she shrugged. "I didn't see it as anything permanent. I sublet my apartment and rented a place here."

"So, what work did you do for him?"

"I set up the microphones and made adjustments to balance the sound. It was very basic since Cooper was an acoustical musician. But, outdoor concerts can be a bit tricky."

"In what way?"

"Well, you have to consider the size of the venue, the size of the crowd, the wind, noise from the surrounding area, things like that," she explained.

"Ms. Wolfson, how would you describe your relationship with Cooper? Was it of a romantic nature?"

Maya vigorously shook her head. "Not at all, Detective. We worked together. We'd go out after a gig sometimes."

"Yes?"

"Well, after a show, we'd go out, sometimes to Fathoms, for a drink. Mostly, we'd talk about what went well, what we needed to do the next time, things like that. Cooper was a very private person--totally opposite from the person the audience saw performing."

"Did you ever go to his apartment?"

"Are you kidding? That place was creepy! I wouldn't set foot in there."

"I'm not talking about that place. Did you know of any other apartment that Cooper had?"

Maya faced Raul across the desk with a wide-eyed look. "Detective, Cooper never had another apartment. I swear."

Raul stared at Maya for several seconds. Every detective knows that you often ask questions to which you already know the answers. And, from the security camera tapes, Raul had evidence that she had visited Cooper's penthouse. "Ms. Wolfson, you need to tell me the truth." Raul leaned his forearms on his desk and looked straight at Maya.

Her eyes filled with tears and she shook her head. "I have no idea what you're talking about. But, it's very hard for me to think of Cooper as dead. Murdered. He was a good guy."

"Well, somebody didn't think so. Why do you think someone would want to kill him?"

Maya shrugged her shoulders as she blew her nose. "No idea, Detective. No idea at all."

Raul waited silently, hoping Maya would fill in the space. Finally, he decided to end the interview. "Ms. Wolfson, you're free to leave, but it's likely that I will need to speak with you further. So, please be available. And, Ms. Wolfson, if you think of anything else that might help us find Cooper's killer, please contact me. Here's my card."

"Of course, Detective. Have a good day."

"You, too, Ms. Wolfson."

It was time to head to Pamela and Ron's sunset cocktail party. Ellen took one last look in her full-length mirror, checking for any wardrobe malfunctions. Last year's outfit still seemed to work: linen skinny jeans, a silk ecru tank and a flowy cardigan. Strappy sandals replaced last year's flip-flops. In an effort to avoid unnecessary bulges, Ellen ate grapefruit for breakfast and skipped lunch entirely. Turning seventy was tough, but seventy-one is a bitch!

Their van was permitted through the gated entrance to Tarpon Point Marina. The one-mile approach to the hotel was even more magnificent than they remembered. The archway of palm trees, lining each side of the road, was taller and thicker this year. Ellen fantasized that they were approaching Jay Gatsby's opulent, Georgian mansion. The gardens framing the entrance of the hotel were a riot of reds and whites, set off by deep, intense green foliage.

Charlie gave their names to the parking attendant who checked them in. The attendant, then, hustled to Ellen's side, opening her door and extending his hand. She and Charlie made their way to Marker 92, the restaurant situated on the promenade, facing the water. The terrace, jutting out towards the marina, was separated from the interior restaurant by two ornate, white columns. A graceful balustrade surrounded the entire terrace. Appropriate attire for this event was Cape Coral casual. Nevertheless, the event was elegant. Men were all wearing neatly pressed, linen slacks with golf shirts. The women had, probably, each, spent the equivalent of a mortgage payment to achieve an air of nonchalance.

As they joined the Gatsby set, Ellen swiftly nabbed a glass of champagne from a server's tray to calm her nerves. "Ellen, Charlie!" a familiar voice called.

"Pamela, wonderful to see you!" Ellen exclaimed. Pamela was dressed in a full-length, flowing white linen dress that moved gracefully as she floated over to greet them.

"You both look fantastic," Pamela said, reaching out to hug Charlie.

"Pamela, you look lovely. It's great to see you again! Ron around?"

Pamela motioned with her head, "He's over at the bar. Go on, Charlie. He'll be thrilled to see you."

Charlie made his way to the bar and before he could get to Ron, Waldorf and Statler, Ron's bankers, flagged him down. They were seated at the very same stools where he met them a year ago.

"Well, well, it's good to see you again." Waldorf extended his hand or was it Statler? Charlie never did know who was who.

"Welcome back!" said the other.

Charlie greeted them both. "Have you, two, been sitting here ever since I last saw you?"

"Probably," one of them said. The other nodded in agreement."

"Charlie, what do you want to drink? It's on me," chuckled Waldorf or was it Statler? "Nasty business about that Cooper murder."

"Sure is," Charlie agreed.

"Well, if you ask me," the other one concluded, "Cooper probably had it coming to him."

"What makes you say that?" Charlie asked.

"Charlie, you don't ever mess around with tough, older women. You're better off taking on the Mafia." He laughed aloud at his own comment.

Charlie was relieved to hear Ron's voice bellowing to him from the other end of the bar, "Hey, there, Charlie! Come on over here!" The two men greeted each other with the hearty slap/hug maneuver. They had formed a friendship based on unconventional circumstances a year ago.

Meanwhile, Pamela took Ellen's arm and led her to her book group friends. Ellen was delighted to see some of the women she had met last year at the party. They all chatted amiably while Pamela excused herself to mingle with her other guests. The conversation, almost immediately, focused on the Cooper murder. These women were passionate fans who felt sad and betrayed, at the same time.

A blond of indeterminate age admitted, "I wouldn't want my husband to know, but I gave Cooper money for that bogus senior music studio fund. In cash! I'm such a fool!"

"Don't feel bad. We were all taken in by him," another woman added.

A server offered them champagne from his tray, which they all accepted without even pausing in their conversation. Ellen took a large swallow of hers and said, "It's not often that women of our age become a hot singer's target audience."

"Here, here!" they toasted, raising their glasses and guzzling their champagne. They began talking about the advantages and disadvantages of arriving at the age of invisibility. They didn't hesitate to indulge, once again, when another server arrived bearing a tray of champagne. As they gulped down the drinks, Ellen included, they chanted loudly, "AND AGE IS NOT A NUMBER!"

Ellen, who was becoming a bit inebriated, remembered, too late, that she hadn't eaten all day. "Ladies, I need to get something to eat. You'll have to excuse me."

"Ellen, try the shrimp. They're delicious. Right over there," one of the women suggested.

Ellen carefully made her way to the shrimp platter, holding onto the balustrade whenever possible in order to remain upright. As she dipped her shrimp into the cocktail sauce, she overheard two women talking next to her. And, Ellen, who always welcomed an opportunity to eavesdrop, pretended to be engrossed in dunking and redunking her shrimp.

"Are you serious?" a woman wearing a low-cut, white gauzy blouse sneered. "He was nothing but a narcissistic con man." She threw her head back and took a swig of her martini.

The woman to whom she spoke, whined, "But, Cooper made me feel beautiful and, well, um..."

85

"Special," Ellen boldly interjected while chewing noisily on her shrimp. She felt delightfully reckless.

"Why, thank-you. Yes, special. That's the word I was looking for. I'm Violet and this is Sharon."

"I'm Ellen." The women shook hands.

"Honestly, I think all of you women are pathetic," Sharon scoffed. "And, besides, Cooper had the IQ of a gnat!"

"Pfft! Who cared about his IQ," Ellen countered. Violet laughed nervously.

"Well, I did!" Sharon retorted. "Besides, what business is this of yours? I was having a private conversation with Violet."

"The shrimp made me do it," Ellen giggled. Regretfully, she was more than a bit 'pompette'. She waved the dunked shrimp at Sharon for emphasis. Unfortunately, the cocktail sauce splattered, leaving Sharon's gauzy white blouse and cleavage speckled in red.

"Sharon, I am so sorry!" Ellen cried, totally mortified by her own behavior. "I feel horrible!"

"It's nothing," Sharon fumed.

Charlie was already heading in Ellen's direction as this scene unfolded and decided it was time to intervene. "Hello, ladies. I'm Ellen's husband, Charlie," he gave a courtly smile and nod. "Please excuse us." Sharon nodded back and stomped off to the ladies' room.

Turning to Ellen, Charlie said, "Sweetie, let's go watch the sunset." He, firmly, put his arm around her to keep her steady and whisked her away. Ellen knew there was nothing she could do to make things right with Sharon. Charlie tried to console her. But, it was the sun that created the distraction they needed as its glow spread across the horizon.

The sunlight was replaced by soft, flickering lanterns that gently illuminated the terrace area. Pamela and Ron had invited Ellen and Charlie to hang around afterwards so they could have a chance to catch up. Ellen, completely sobered by the shrimp fiasco, was desperate to speak privately with Pamela. She described spraying the cocktail sauce and how she wanted to do something to make it up to Sharon.

"You must mean Sharon Thompson. Tall, lots of cleavage, white blouse, unpleasant?"

Ellen nodded. "That's gotta be her."

"She and her husband, Eli, are prominent Cape Coral residents. He's a proctologist and Sharon is, well, she's a social climber."

"Pamela, could you please give me her address? The only thing I can think to do is to send her some flowers. I'm so embarrassed."

"I'll text you her address, but, really, Sharon is probably infuriated with someone else by now." Pamela rolled her eyes. "I wouldn't worry about it."

"Thanks."

"But, I am a little miffed, Ellen. Sharon was dripping in cocktail sauce and I missed the whole thing!"

On the ride home Charlie asked, "What were you and that woman arguing about when I came by?"

"Nothing really. She said that I butted into her conversation. Can you believe that, Charlie? Really? Me?"

"Hard to imagine, Sweetie," Charlie smiled to himself.

Saturday, March 9

Ellen and Charlie had just put away their Farmers' Market produce and were about to enjoy their almond croissants and coffee on the lanai. Ellen's phone "can-canned". It was Ginger.

"Hi Ginger! Good to hear from you. What's up?"

"Ellen, hi. Look, I can't talk long. Our grandkids are visiting this weekend."

"That's great, Ginger."

"No, it's not great, Ellen. Not great at all," Ginger said becoming agitated. "You see, Hugh thought our two-year-old and four-year-old grandsons would have fun playing with the Styrofoam packing that our new TV came in. But, I know that's not really why he gave them the Styrofoam. Hugh did this so they would be busy and he could bond with the remote and watch the Arnold Palmer Invitational today without being disturbed."

"So, that sounds like a win-win for everyone. Big deal," Ellen reasoned.

"Well, Ellen, let me just say that right now the inside of my house looks like a Styrofoam blizzard!" Ginger screeched.

"Ginger, what did you say? I can hardly hear you." Ellen yelled, perplexed, "What the heck is all that noise in the background?"

Ginger shouted back, "It's the vacuum cleaner. I have to help Hugh vacuum off the kids."

"Vacuum off the kids? Seriously, Ginger?" Ellen was flabbergasted.

Ginger gritted her teeth and snapped, "Yes, Ellen. Vacuum off the kids! But, here's why I called. I need you to check up again on my friend's mother, Beverly Miller."

"I did that a couple of times, Ginger, and she's really a smart, independent sort. I don't think Laura has a thing to worry about."

"I hope you're right. Laura said that her mother is very involved in the murder of that singer, Cooper. I think that was his name."

"What are you talking about?"

"Well, Laura said that her mother has been questioned several times by a young detective. He contacts her almost every day for more information and seems to think she has a lot of information to share."

"You're talking about Detective Sergeant Swann. I find that very hard to believe, Ginger."

"Exactly. That's why I need--Laura needs--you to visit her mom again. Please check out what's going on. Laura is frantic that her mother may have witnessed something and could be in grave danger."

"Tell Laura to sit tight. I'll go over later this morning. Fortunately, today is Beverly's day off," Ellen said glibly.

"Her day off?"

"Yes. Saturday is the one day she doesn't play tennis."

Ginger was speechless. Finally, she said, "Call me later. Gotta run!"

After a quick breakfast, Ellen rode her bike to Beverly's home and waited for her to answer the door.

"Oh, it's you," Beverly said. "Why are you here?"

"Really, Beverly, you think I'm here to sell you Girl Scout cookies?" Ellen replied sarcastically. "I was taking a bike ride and thought I'd stop by to say 'hi'."

"Okay. You might as well come in. Coffee?"

"Love some. Thanks."

Beverly reheated her leftover coffee in the microwave and brought it out to the lanai for the two of them.

"So, besides kicking everyone's butt on the tennis court, what have you been up to?" Ellen asked.

"Oh, don't even ask!" Beverly sighed in exasperation.

"Well, I already did ask. So, what have you been up to?"

Beverly spoke softly as if she were divulging an important secret. "Well, I've barely had time to play tennis, Ellen. That nice detective who came to see me after Cooper, well, you know, after Cooper was--ahem, killed, he gave me his card and told me to call him any time--any time--if I remembered anything that could help him find the murderer."

"And did you?"

"Of course. I was, simply, performing my civic duty."

"What information did you have, Beverly?"

"I recalled bits of our dinner conversation. And, every time I called him, Detective Swann was most appreciative," Beverly asserted.

"Every time?"

"Yes, practically every day." Ellen's look of shock served only to egg Beverly on. "Oh, yes! I remembered what Cooper had for dinner that night. Another time, I recalled that Cooper's favorite musician was John Lennon. And, then, I remembered that someone came over to our table to ask for his autograph."

"And, who was that?"

"I have no idea. Some woman around your age," Beverly said, eyeing Ellen critically. "And, Cooper signed her napkin quickly. He didn't like to be recognized in public, you see."

Beverly went on to explain, "I told all of this to that charming detective in person, every time."

"I thought you called him?"

"Ellen, you can be so naive! You can't trust that phone calls are private. I only called to arrange to meet Detective Swann."

"And, where did you meet?"

Beverly came as close to a giggle as she, probably, ever had. "Right where you're sitting. On this very lanai. Of course, a couple of times, I showed up at the police station. Ellen," she whispered, "I've become vital to this investigation. Do you realize that? Detective Swann practically said as much. He really is so handsome! Have you met him?"

Ellen nodded. "I do happen to know Detective Swann--very well, in fact. I ran into him as I was leaving your place the day after the murder. We became friends last year. So, we are quite well-acquainted," Ellen smiled smugly. She found that Beverly triggered competitive instincts she never realized she possessed.

"Oh. He's a very busy man, but always makes time for me," Beverly added, attempting to top Ellen. "My tennis group is positively envious of me. I love it! And, it's not just that I whip their butts on the tennis court. They all understand that I am playing an important role in this case. It's becoming a little tiresome, but after tennis, now, we go to the Boat House so I can tell them, discreetly of course, about my latest interrogation." Beverly chuckled, "Do you realize, Ellen, that they argue over who gets to pay for my lunch. Might as well start ordering the lobster roll!" she snickered.

Ellen shook her head in amazement.

"You're going to have to leave soon. Detective Swann is coming to see me."

"Why would he be stopping to see you on a Saturday?" Ellen was becoming irritated with Beverly's air of self-importance.

"Something else that I remembered. That's all," she said mysteriously.

"Yes?"

"Ellen, I couldn't possibly tell you. It's confidential police information."

"Well, you seem to have no problem telling your entire tennis group! How confidential do you think that is?" Ellen shot back.

"Well, if you insist," Beverly relented. "Cooper told me that he had just signed a recording deal. And, he was going to record an entire album of his original songs."

"Oh, my God! Beverly, that, actually, is a very useful bit of information."

"You sound surprised," Beverly snapped.

Ellen replied, "Not at all, Beverly. I'm impressed. By the way, your daughter is frantic. She thinks you might be in danger."

"So, that's why you're here, isn't it?" Ellen nodded. "Well, I may have exaggerated when I talked to her, just a bit."

"Just a bit? Laura is convinced that you witnessed something, and the murderer is hunting you down!"

"Oh, Laura gets upset so easily. All I said was that I was one of the last people to see Cooper alive and it wouldn't surprise me if the murderer was someone watching us that evening. He might even have been following us back here."

Ellen's eyes narrowed as she said, "Well, it's no wonder that Laura is worried! Is that the same story you told to your tennis friends and to Detective Swann?"

Beverly shrugged in response.

"I will call and let your daughter know that you are perfectly safe. But, if you keep telling lies, I'm going to spill the beans to Detective Swann and to your tennis group and it will be a separate check for you at the Boat House from now on!"

Ellen marched to the door to let herself out. Beverly looked in the mirror and puckered her lips to see if she needed to reapply her lipstick.

That evening, Catherine and Ted drove to the Barbara B. Mann Theatre with Ellen and Charlie. This impressive performing arts center is located in Fort Myers on the campus of Florida Southwestern State College, just over the bridge from Cape Coral. The theatre seats almost two thousand and is a choice venue for Broadway touring groups as well as classical music concerts, dance performances, and various other entertainment. Tonight they were going to be treated to a performance by "Tap Dogs". The performers, literally, create a construction site on the stage. The show illustrates the "power of workmen with the precision and talent of tap dancing".

Before the house lights were turned off, a woman seemed to be walking in their direction from the front of the theatre. It looked very much like Sharon with the cocktail sauce cleavage. Ellen was embarrassed. She turned her head away from the aisle, towards Catherine, to avoid being recognized. But, much to Ellen's dismay, Sharon stopped right in front of them.

"Sharon, how nice to see you," Catherine greeted her. They both air-kissed.

"Good to see you, too, Catherine."

"I'd like you to meet..."

Sharon interrupted, "No need for introductions," she said frostily. "You're Ellen." Ellen nodded.

"I see you two have already met. Anyhow, Sharon, hope to see you at water aerobics one of these days," Catherine said.

"I hope so. Better get back to my seat. Just wanted to say, 'hello'. Ta-ta!" With one more air-kiss and an aloof nod to Ellen, Sharon ta-taed herself back to her third row, center seat.

"What's the story with you and Sharon? That was awkward," Catherine said, stating the obvious.

Ellen recapped the shrimp cocktail gaffe. "So, you know her from water aerobics?"

"Sort of. She shows up occasionally, when she's between galas and art show openings. She and her husband are big-time patrons of the

Performing Arts Center," Catherine explained. "The only thing real about Sharon is her vanity."

Sharon found that Ellen woman dreadfully irritating, but, lately, she found everyone irritating. She silently slid into her seat next to Eli, sitting as far away from him as possible.

Sunday, March 10

Sharon was drinking her coffee and reading the paper. She could hear Eli noisily crunching away on his high fiber breakfast at the other end of the lanai. This was the most she had heard out of Eli in a month. When the doorbell rang, Sharon rose to answer it. Standing in front of her was that Ellen woman holding an extravagant bouquet of flowers.

Sharon looked at her quizzically, "Yes?"

"Hello, Sharon. I feel so bad about the other night--the cocktail sauce. I wanted to bring you these," Ellen offered, presenting the bouquet to Sharon.

"You really didn't need to do that but thank-you. Please come in. Would you like some coffee?"

"If it's not any trouble."

"What do you like in it?"

"I take it black," Ellen replied. She entered a contemporary home that seemed to be built, entirely, of glass. Everywhere she looked included a breathtaking water view. The art and minimalist furniture exuded elegance and class. Ellen had run by this home almost every day, but had no idea how magnificent it was from the inside. "Sharon, you've created a beautiful home!" Ellen exclaimed.

"Thank-you," Sharon said matter-of-factly as she led the way to the lanai. "Eli, I'd like you to meet Ellen. She and I met at the Green's party on Friday."

98

Eli got up, looked at his Rolex, and shook hands politely. "Nice to meet you. You'll have to excuse me. I have to get going."

As soon as her husband left, Sharon asked Ellen, "So, how do you know Pamela and Ron Green?"

"My husband and I met them last winter. They helped us solve the Jack Newman murder."

"Oh? That's interesting. The Jack Newman murder. It had the entire community on edge. And, you say, that you and your husband helped to solve it?" Sharon replied, clearing her throat.

Ellen was quite sure that she noticed Sharon's right hand trembling ever so slightly as she handed Ellen a cup and saucer. However, Ellen merely nodded, "Isn't it strange that, here we are one year later and, there's been another murder in Cape Coral?"

"Yes, but someone like Cooper probably had it coming."

"Really? He seemed so charming and had so many devoted fans," Ellen replied.

"There's another side to that story," said Sharon cryptically.

"What do you mean?"

"Well, you already know that he was scamming all of those women. And, then, there were the jealous husbands, of course."

"Instead of being jealous," Ellen surmised, "you'd think they'd see it as a wake-up call and pay more attention to their wives."

Sharon raised her eyebrows. "I'm afraid it didn't work that way. There are lots of husbands who are very happy that Cooper was killed."

"There are?"

"Let me put it this way: Eli isn't exactly in mourning over Cooper's death," Sharon whispered. "But, what can I say. Cooper was Cooper."

"So, you knew Cooper fairly well?"

Sharon shrugged her shoulders. "I was involved with several of his fund-raisers, but I kept my distance. I never trusted him."

"Then, you were smarter than most women," Ellen concluded.

"Hmmph," Sharon muttered. "It was very obvious what Cooper was all about: himself." Sharon clenched her jaw tightly. "He was a user, that's all."

"Did you feel betrayed by him? Because of his phony music fund, I mean." Ellen inquired.

Sharon seemed offended by the question. "Of course not. I never trusted the bastard." Sharon's voice had an angry edge to it.

"Didn't mean to pry, but I'm curious about what Cooper was like."

"It doesn't matter what he was like. He's gone and good riddance," Sharon said indifferently.

Neither woman spoke for a couple of minutes. They both pretended to be drinking their coffee. Finally, Ellen knew that, by now, Charlie would be pushing her out the door before she owed Sharon another bouquet of flowers. She reached out to shake Sharon's hand. "Thanks for the coffee, Sharon. Again, I'm so sorry about the other night. I better be on my way. I don't want to hold you up anymore," Ellen smiled as she stood up to leave. "Please enjoy the flowers."

"Thank-you." The women exchanged a cordial good-bye.

On her way home, Ellen decided to stop by to see Catherine. Catherine had been watering the vegetable garden out back. With the sun directly overhead, they sat in the shaded patio area and sipped iced tea. "Wasn't that an amazing performance last night?" Catherine began.

"It made me want to tap my way home!" Ellen agreed.

"Okay, Ellen. You're here for a reason. What is it?" Catherine wasted no time in getting to the point.

"You're right. I was wondering about Sharon. What do you know about her?"

"Not much, really. Like I said, she would occasionally show up at water aerobics, but hasn't been there for months now."

"Did she ever mention Cooper?"

Catherine snickered, "Mention him? She was obsessed with Cooper!"

"You're kidding."

"It got to be so annoying," Catherine continued. "Karen and I were really happy when she stopped showing up to class."

"Why? What things did she say about Cooper?"

"A lot of nonsense. It was all about her, surprise, surprise," Catherine rolled her eyes. "About how beautiful Cooper thought she was. Who says things like that?" Catherine grumbled.

"Wow! And, now she trashes him every chance she gets," Ellen replied, puzzled.

"That's strange. In fact, we were all convinced that she and Cooper were having an affair."

"No way!"

"Oh, yeah! Sharon bragged about her private lunches with him and secret meetings."

"I don't imagine her husband was happy about it!"

"Eli? Pfft. He could care less about what Sharon was up to. Besides, Eli was totally oblivious. He had his head up his--you-know-what!" Catherine and Ellen shrieked with laughter like a couple of teenagers.

"I better head back home," Ellen giggled, "before Charlie sends out a search party!"

By late afternoon, Ellen and Charlie headed to the Cape Harbour Marina where they indulged in one of their favorite tourist attractions: the Banana Bay Sunset Cruise. First Mate Andy was already shmoozing with the passengers as they boarded the boat. Tonight was to be his very last cruise before his retirement. And, Andy was determined to make the most of it. He regaled the passengers with the riotous story of how he met his wife a few years ago. Apparently, she had been one of the passengers and it was love at first sight, as Andy described it. For Andy's final cruise, Denise, his wife, was on board, seated in the rear of the boat. She was laughing and blushing as Andy spared few details of their unconventional courtship.

Captain J.R. Tremper, owner of the Banana Bay Tour Company, piloted the boat. As a naturalist, he was able to expertly field questions from passengers of all ages. Captain J.R. was adept at locating areas where dolphins were cavorting. He pointed out eagles' nests, white pelicans and, of course, positioned the boat to show off a flamboyant sunset. Throughout the spectacular ninety-minute cruise, he and Andy bantered back and forth. It was obvious that the two had developed an easy, spirited repartee over the years. The ending of the cruise was bittersweet as Captain and First Mate completed their final voyage together.

Much later, it was a perfect hot tub evening for Ellen and Charlie. The night air had a slight chill as the temperature dipped into the sixties. But the colored light show and the steam coming up from the tub lured them right in. As had become their custom, Ellen got in first and Charlie followed with two glasses of sauvignon blanc. For the first few minutes, the water gushing out of the jets and the clink of glasses were the only sounds to be heard. Then, Ellen broke the silence. "Charlie, this morning, I brought some flowers to that woman, Sharon. You know, the one I sprayed with cocktail sauce?"

Charlie nodded. "I'm sure she was thrilled to see you," he said sarcastically.

"That doesn't matter. But, I got conflicting stories. Listen to this. Sharon has done nothing but bad-mouth Cooper, yet, Catherine said that Sharon was obsessed with him. She and Karen thought they were having an affair!"

"Ellen, who cares? Cooper is dead."

"Charlie, don't you get it? Cooper probably used her like he used lots of women and she hated him for doing that to her."

"Ellen, I see where you're going with this and I think it's all a lot of conjecture and rumor," Charlie warned.

"Charlie, bottom line is that we now know of three people who hated Cooper: Frank Blake who got screwed out of his inheritance and that guy who plays racquetball with Bud."

"You mean Eli, Eli Thompson? Ellen, he was just grumbling. I'm sure he wasn't serious."

104

"Wait a minute. Eli Thompson? I'll bet that's the same Eli Thompson I met this morning: the proctologist and he's married to Sharon Thompson, Charlie."

"Yeah. So?"

"Well, they both seem to be a couple of hot-heads as soon as Cooper's name comes up. That's all," Ellen said smugly.

"Okay, Miss Marple, what's next?" Charlie gave Ellen his I-don't-like-this-but-I can't-hold-back-the-river look.

Monday, March 11

Captain McConnell had scheduled a meeting with Detective Swann. New information had been confirmed regarding Cooper, A.K.A. Mark Simmons. A phone number on Cooper's mobile phone had been traced to a Ned Abbott from El Paso. "Our counterparts in El Paso located this Ned Abbott and brought him in for questioning," Raul began. "Abbott was shocked to learn that Cooper had been murdered. They had talked a few weeks ago."

"How did they meet?" McConnell asked.

"They met back in El Paso in the early '80's one summer. They were both musicians and jammed together, occasionally. Their music seemed to be the connection between them."

"What kind of contact did they have over the years?" McConnell asked.

"Abbott said that when Cooper disappeared in '89, he would call Ned from pay phones every so often to check in. These were pre-mobile phone days," Raul reminded the Captain.

"Swann, I am well aware of that, thank-you!" McConnell retorted.

"Sorry, Sir. I'll continue." Raul cleared his throat and resumed his update. "They stayed in touch and even met up to jam together occasionally over the last ten to fifteen years. Austin, Chicago, Atlanta, here and there."

"So, what was the most recent phone call about? You said that was a few weeks ago."

106

"According to Abbott, Cooper invited him to come to Cape Coral for a visit. He told Abbott that it would be fun. They could hang out with their old songwriter friend who moved to town last April." Raul paused. "Captain McConnell, the friend's name, by the way, is Maya Wolfson," Raul stated.

"Swann, get her back in for questioning. Pronto! She lied to us to cover up something and you need to find out what it is."

"Ms. Wolfson, I appreciate your coming in on such short notice," Raul said. "Does the name Ned Abbott mean anything to you?"

Maya's left leg began to vibrate and she stared at Raul. "I'm not sure, Detective. What was the name again?"

"Ned Abbott."

"Hmm, that sounds familiar."

"Ms. Wolfson, I'm going to cut to the chase. Tell me about your history with Ned Abbott and with Cooper. Or did you know Cooper by another name?" Raul folded his arms and waited for Maya's response.

"Like I said the other day, I was the sound-tech for Cooper."

"Ned Abbott," Raul refocused her. "Tell me about you, Ned Abbott, and Cooper."

"Alright, but there really isn't much to tell," she sighed. "We all met years ago at a bar in Austin. It was open-mic night and we decided to team up for fun."

"Go on."

"I sang and they played guitar. Mark, I mean Cooper, sang with me. He had a sexy voice and he won over the crowds."

"So, you all stayed in touch through the years?"

Maya nodded. "Somewhat. We were good for each other, musically, that is. We began writing our own songs. Well, I shouldn't say 'we'. Ned was really the songwriter. Wrote a lot of good stuff."

"Interesting, Ms. Wolfson. He said that you were the songwriter. Why would he say that?"

"Haven't a clue, Detective. But I wish I had that talent. My singing, alone, sure doesn't do it," she said glibly.

"Ms. Wolfson, why did you lie to me about knowing Cooper? Last Friday, you told me that you met him a year ago." Raul stared intently at her from across the desk.

"I was afraid and didn't want to get involved."

"And is that why you lied about going to his penthouse, too?"

Maya shrugged and couldn't bring herself to look at Raul.

"And are you lying when you say that it was Ned who was the songwriter? Ms. Wolfson, please answer the question."

108

Maya suddenly sat up straight and, without wavering said, "Why don't you ask Ned Abbott why he said I was the songwriter, Detective. He's the liar, not me."

"What are you trying to hide?"

Maya's eyes filled with tears. "I just don't want to be involved. That's all. Do you blame me?"

"When did you last see Cooper?"

"Saturday, at the Farmers' Market. I set up the microphones and helped him pack up his equipment."

"Did you see him after Saturday?" Raul asked, knowing full well that she had.

"Detective Swann, I just told you that I saw him on Saturday for his performance," Maya said impatiently.

"Ms. Wolfson, do you realize that you are putting yourself in a very compromising position?"

"What do you mean, Detective?"

"Do you really want me to show you the security camera footage of you exiting Cooper's Crimson Court apartment building very late Monday evening, February 25th?" Raul stated matter-of-factly. "Now, why don't you make it easier on yourself and tell me what you were doing there at 11:42 P.M."

Maya stared directly at Raul and responded, "I needed to pick up a small microphone from him for another gig I had coming up that week."

"Really? At that hour?" Raul looked skeptically at Maya.

"Yes, Detective. Cooper and I worked together. Period. I was on my way home and texted to see if I could stop by. But you already knew about my text, right?" Maya asked sarcastically.

Raul simply raised his eyebrows and continued his questioning. "Ms. Wolfson, you persist in lying to me. Why?"

Maya shrugged, "I already told you, Detective. I'm afraid of getting involved."

"Well, Ms. Wolfson, it's a little late to worry about getting involved. You are involved!" Raul fired back at her. "Now, it's time you started telling me the truth--the whole truth." Raul folded his arms and leaned towards her.

Maya looked across the desk at Raul and said, "Okay, so I was in his condo for probably ten minutes. No more."

Raul let the silence uncomfortably fill the room as he fixed his eyes intently on Maya. "Please tell me where you were on Tuesday, February 26th between ten and eleven P.M."

"Are you serious? You think I killed Cooper?"

"Ms. Wolfson, please answer the question," Raul stated firmly.

"Well, I really don't remember."

"Try!"

Maya sat perfectly still without saying a word. Finally, she said, "I may have been home, but I'm not positive."

"Ms. Wolfson, you must realize that we will learn the truth. And, for your sake, I hope we learn it from you." Raul took a deep breath before dismissing Maya. "You're free to leave. But, I ask you to please be available. I'm sure we'll be meeting again."

It was pizza night at Maria's and the big round table was awaiting them, as usual. Rory, their server, didn't even bother taking orders. He showed up with their beverages and had already put in their pizza orders. Ted, Bud, and Charlie were talking about the spring training baseball season. Catherine and Karen were telling Ellen about the water aerobics class that morning.

"So, guess who showed up for the first time in months," Catherine threw out.

"Sharon?"

"Yes, and she went right over to Catherine to give her one of these," Karen said, squinting her eyes and puffing out her lips and chin.

Ellen laughed at this comical impersonation of an air-kiss .

Catherine continued, "She seemed to be much more subdued than I remember, thank God! And, she seemed genuinely grief-stricken about Cooper."

"You must be kidding! How did Cooper even come up in conversation?"

Karen admitted, "I brought him up. After hearing her gush and brag about her little trysts with Cooper, I had to say something."

"Wait a minute. Sharon seemed upset about his death? That doesn't make sense." Ellen was puzzled.

"Oh, yes!" Karen declared. "She went on and on about what a special person Cooper was. What a devoted fan she was. Of course, keep in mind that we were exercising in the deep end of the pool at the time, so I may have missed some of what she said."

"It was ridiculous," Catherine chimed in. "I wanted to vomit!"

"Well, you shut her up in a hurry, didn't you, Catherine?" Karen concluded.

"Catherine, what did you say?" Ellen asked.

"Not much. I just said, 'Cooper must have been pretty special to con you out of your husband's money.' "

Ellen had tears streaming down her face from laughing. "And, what did Sharon say?"

"Nothing. What could she possibly say? She just turned her back to me, gave a little kick, and noodled her way to the other side of the pool."

Tuesday, March 12

Stella quickly threw on some clothes and went to answer her front door. "I'll be right there!" she shouted. The bell rang again. "I'm coming!" Stella called out to the impatient visitor. She opened the door and was face-to-face with Frank Blake, Mildred's son.

"Frank, how nice to see you. Please come in."

"Stella," he nodded. Frank was looking disheveled in his shorts and stained tee shirt. His sunglasses and scruffy beard did nothing to improve his appearance.

"How about some coffee?"

"Don't bother, Stella."

"Well, come sit down on the lanai," Stella suggested uneasily.

"I prefer to stand right here. I'll be very brief," Frank stated brusquely. "Look here, Stella, some friend of yours stopped by my house last week."

"Oh, and who was that?"

"Ellen," Frank gritted his teeth as he said her name.

"Frank, I don't know an Ellen."

"Well, she seemed to know you pretty well."

Stella looked at him, puzzled. "Anyhow, what did this Ellen say to you?"

"She told me that she knew my mother. And, then, she said my mother told her Cooper was like a second son to her."

"Well, this woman was probably just trying to be kind..."

"No, it was the way she said it. Don't patronize me." He cut her off mid-sentence. "This woman was baiting me. I could tell." Frank moved in close to Stella and continued, "She knew about my mother's will. I'm sure she did! And, I'm sure that you're the one who told her." Frank glared at Stella.

"Frank, I swear, I didn't tell anyone!" she insisted. "Really!"

"You're a liar. Besides, if it wasn't for you, my mother would never have changed her will in the first place. I'm warning you, Stella: you better tell your miserable friend to mind her own business."

Stella felt her heart racing and, instinctively, backed away from Frank. She was afraid to speak. Frank strode out the door, turned back to Stella and shook his finger at her. "Don't make me come back here again, Stella!"

Wednesday, March 13

Charlie sauntered into the Boat House for coffee feeling light-hearted. He and Ellen had planned to relax and enjoy the Cape Coral area for the entire day. They had both decided to head to Matlacha.

Matlacha (pronounced, "MAT-la-shay") is known as the "Key West of the North". Today it is a vibrant arts community with brightly colored boutiques, restaurants, galleries, and cottages. With a population of approximately seven hundred, Matlacha residents vow to never have a traffic light.

The village was originally formed in 1926 when Lee County purchased a bridge that connected the Mangrove Islands and Cape Coral. To construct the bridge, they dredged fill from Matlacha Pass. This fill became Matlacha Island. In 1929, people who lost their homes in the stock market crash built shacks and became squatters on the "Fill". These people, mostly commercial fishermen, needed to completely change their livelihood when gill netting was banned in 1990. Thus, they began to embrace the arts, which embodies the essence of present-day Matlacha.

Right after Ellen and Charlie crossed over the Matlacha bridge, they parked the van and began strolling around the village. Ellen, who normally would prefer to go naked rather than ever wear pink, bought a shocking pink ankle bracelet and a pair of shocking pink flip-flops. She paid for them, ripped off the tags, and paraded around in her new look. Charlie, too, got into the Matlacha spirit and bought a neon yellow hat and matching tee shirt. They were enjoying feeling free, funky, and foolish.

116

They decided to head to Bert's Bar and Grill for lunch. The unpretentious dockside restaurant is one of Matlacha's treasures with quite a colorful past. Today, the restaurant boasts fresh seafood, dockside dining at the fishing marina, and live music. The patio area is filled with picnic tables overlooking the water.

Ellen and Charlie sat at a table under a large umbrella and waited for the server to come over. Ellen was suddenly ravenous as she eyed trays of food walking past her. She and Charlie both ordered grouper platters. While they waited for their lunch to arrive, they took in the laid-back ambiance. The musician, a strikingly handsome man with dreadlocks, was playing some Bob Marley music on his steel drum, which only added to the anything-goes feel of the place. After a hearty round of applause, the singer announced a special treat. He was going to accompany his sound-tech person, who was a singer/songwriter when she wasn't working sound. She was going to sing one of her original songs. "Everyone, please give a warm welcome to--Maya Wolfson!"

"Charlie, that's the young woman I was speaking with at Slate's!" Ellen exclaimed. "Remember?"

"Vaguely," Charlie replied.

"She did sound work for Cooper, but I never knew she was a songwriter."

They listened as Maya crooned a haunting, Edith Piaf-style ballad. The diners loved it. Maya bowed, thanked everyone, and left the stage area. As she wound her way through the dining patio, she was flagged down by Ellen who was waving madly. "Maya!" Ellen cried. "You're amazing!"

"Oh, I remember you. Slate's. At the bar. Right?"

Ellen nodded. "That's right. Please sit down and join us."

"Well, just for a couple of minutes. Thanks. You really liked the song?" Maya asked.

"Maya, it was poetry. I loved it!" Ellen answered.

Charlie, in the meantime, got the server's attention and insisted that Maya order something to eat. He thought she looked like she could use a decent meal. "You're a very talented songwriter. I must say. By the way, we're Ellen and Charlie Green." Charlie reached across the table to shake her hand.

The three of them chatted while they enjoyed their meals. "So, Maya," Charlie began as his fork cut into the flaky grouper, "you do have a gift for songwriting, you realize."

"Thanks, Charlie," Maya shrugged modestly. "I enjoy doing it."

Ellen asked, "Have you been writing for a long time?"

"Well," Maya explained, "I started back when I was living in Austin. Everyone there thinks they're a musical prodigy," she laughed.

"Have you recorded any of your songs?" Ellen asked.

"No. It was more important for me to focus on making enough money to live on."

"Do you get many opportunities to sing like you did today?"

"Are you kidding me? Almost never."

"I know you worked for Cooper. What did you think of the songs he wrote?" Ellen asked, recalling her most recent conversation with Beverly.

Maya stopped chewing and looked at Ellen in surprise. "Cooper?" she snickered. "He couldn't write a song if his life depended on it." She resumed eating.

"Really?" Ellen mused, "Well, what happens if someone, like this musician today, were to steal your song?"

"I guess I'd have to kill him," she said, simply, aggressively sinking her teeth into a clam strip.

Ellen suddenly stood up and announced, "Excuse me. I need to find the ladies' room." She grabbed her purse, waited until the ladies' room was free, and pulled out her phone. She scrolled through her contacts and placed a phone call.

"Hello."

"Hello, Beverly, it's Ellen Green."

"Ellen, I'm not a dottering old lady. Of course, I know it's you. I added you to my phone as one of my contacts. What is it? Did my daughter put you up to this again?"

"Beverly, sorry. No. This has nothing to do with Laura. I have a quick question."

"Okay."

"Did you tell me that Cooper was excited about signing a record deal?"

"Oh, so you do listen, don't you," Beverly stated.

"Only when absolutely necessary," Ellen replied, annoyed by Beverly's comment.

"Well, he told me, in confidence of course, that he had just signed this deal and was going to produce an album."

"Beverly, do you recall, did Cooper say that this was to be an album of his original songs?"

"Ellen, but of course. That's exactly what he said. It was to be an album of his original songs: 'Cooper originals', he called them. Why bother to produce an album of Sinatra songs that Sinatra already sang--and a whole lot better?"

"How foolish of me. Listen, one more question, Beverly. Did you tell Detective Swann about this record deal?"

"I had planned to tell him, but he left me a voicemail and told me he couldn't stop by that day--that was Saturday. Anyhow, I was a bit put off by his cancelling on me and haven't gotten around to telling him yet. It can wait," Beverly said indifferently.

"Beverly, thanks. I'll be in touch."

"Bye, Ellen. Oh, and do give Laura my best!" Beverly always managed to get in the last word. Ellen felt irritated, outwitted, and in awe of this exasperating woman.

As she meandered back to the table, Ellen's mind was on fast-forward. Charlie, in the meantime, was engrossed in his conversation. "I imagine there's a code of ethics among musicians, isn't there?" Charlie asked. Maya shrugged and greedily attacked another clam.

Charlie didn't know what was going on with Ellen, but this, definitely, was not the first time he had to step in and steer against the undertow. "So, Maya, where are you going to be working next?"

Maya chattered easily about her next few gigs. They all devoured their food and enjoyed the last set of music. When the server brought the check, Charlie grabbed it before it even hit the table. Maya thanked Charlie and left to help pack up the sound equipment.

In the van on the ride home, Ellen glanced down at her feet in shock. The bright pink flip-flops and ankle bracelet that she had thought were so funky now looked ridiculous. She planned to take them off the moment they got home. Charlie, on the other hand, didn't seem a bit disturbed that he was wearing a neon yellow hat and matching shirt. He was just singing away, totally uninhibited.

"Charlie, I need to talk to you about Maya."

"Sure, Sweetie. It was fun to speak with her and I really enjoyed her song."

"Me, too, but..."

"But, now are you going to tell me what was going on at lunch?" Charlie inquired.

"You could tell something was going on?" Ellen was genuinely surprised. "I thought I was being so discreet."

"Hah! Discreet? You? Ellen, you are many things, but discreet is not one of them."

Ellen sighed, "Alright, here's what happened." She explained the information that Beverly confirmed for her.

"So, wait a minute. You think that Cooper was stealing Maya's songs, planning to record them for his record deal, and claiming them as his own?"

Ellen nodded, "Yes, that's exactly what I think."

"Poor Maya!"

"Poor Maya? Charlie, Maya may have had a motive for killing Cooper! Don't you get it?"

"Ellen, I don't buy that at all," Charlie said dismissively. "I don't see Maya as a murderer."

"Well, maybe you don't but I wonder if Detective Sergeant Raul Swann will."

"You're going to get in touch with Raul?"

"Yes, I am and you're coming with me," Ellen stated definitively.

That evening, Maya tried calling Ned Abbott. When he didn't answer, she left a brief message: "Ned, you know who this is. You need to get in touch with me as soon as possible!" She hung up and, immediately, regretted making the call, but it was too late.

After lunch, Charlie, reluctantly, accompanied Ellen to the police station. The desk sergeant told them that Detective Swann had a few minutes before his next appointment and would be happy to meet with them. She escorted Ellen and Charlie to Raul's office.

"Ellen, Charlie." Raul greeted them with hugs as he showed them in.

"This is quite a step up, Raul!" Charlie said as he surveyed Raul's new digs. "Your promotion has its perks, I see."

"Jennifer reminds me that, now, I have to live up to my new office," Raul smiled. "How have you been, Charlie?"

"Great. And Ellen tells me that you and Jennifer are expecting a baby in September."

Raul beamed and nodded. "Hmm, I'm pretty sure that this is not a social visit. Right, Ellen?"

"We always love to see you, but, yes, you're right," she admitted.

"And, it wouldn't have anything to do with the Cooper murder, would it?" Raul correctly assumed.

"Well, Sherlock, I can, certainly, see why you were promoted," Ellen shot right back.

"Alright, Ellen, why don't you tell me what you've been up to," Raul said mischievously.

"Okay. Let me get right to the point. Beverly Miller..."

"Oh, Mrs. Miller," he interrupted. "Yes. She told me she thinks I'm cute!"

"Well, Raul, I think she's over that now," Ellen said brusquely. "Anyhow, Beverly remembered that Cooper was excited about a recording contract he had just signed. He was going to record an entire album of his original songs."

"Okay."

"And, yesterday, when Charlie and I were having lunch with Maya Wolfson, she..."

"Wait a minute. You had lunch with Maya Wolfson!" Raul exclaimed. "How the heck do you know Maya Wolfson?"

"Please, Raul. Let me finish. Maya performed one of her original songs at a restaurant in Matlacha. Afterwards, she joined us for lunch and talked about her songwriting. Bottom line: Maya said that Cooper wasn't capable of writing a song. And, she said that if anyone stole one of her songs and claimed it as his own," Ellen paused for dramatic effect, "she would have to kill him!"

Charlie jumped right in. "Ellen, she wasn't saying that literally. She was trying to make a point."

"Maybe or maybe not, Charlie," Ellen retorted.

"What is going on?" Raul heaved a heavy sigh and continued. "How do you, two, do it? You're always three steps ahead of me. First, you get the one and only bit of valuable info from Beverly that she has.

125

Second, you, somehow, are onto Maya Wolfson AND you have the proof that she writes songs."

There was a knock at the door. "Detective Swann, your visitor is waiting."

"Thanks, Sergeant Drake. Please ask her to have a seat. I'll be with her in a few minutes." Raul scratched his head. "I'm glad you passed this along to me. Right now, I don't know whether to tell you to butt out of this or..."

"Yes, Raul, or what?" Ellen asked.

"Or whether I need you to keep digging for more."

Ellen smiled at this. "Raul, you know that you need us. We can get people to talk. But, I need you to tell me what you know about Maya."

"Not much, I'm afraid. But, you're right. You need to be informed in order to help move this investigation forward."

Charlie asked, "You don't really think Maya murdered Cooper, do you?"

"Charlie, I really don't know. I do know that I've brought her in for questioning and she lied to me. She said she met Cooper a year ago and, then, she grudgingly admitted that she knew him back in Austin, years before."

"She probably didn't want to get involved," Charlie surmised.

"You may be right, but that's not the only lie she told me. She denied that she writes songs. She's lied about a number of things," Raul admitted cautiously. "She's, definitely, hiding something and I need to find out what that is."

"We'll do our best," Ellen offered eagerly. "Right, Charlie?"

"Look, I think you're going in the wrong direction with this. I really do. But, I suppose, Raul, if you think we can be of help, I can't turn my back on you. You've helped us out in the past."

Raul smiled. "Thanks, Charlie. Just keep me informed about what you learn. I would never put you and Ellen in a dangerous situation. Please believe that."

"I know that, Raul. We'll do what we can." Charlie and Raul shook hands.

"Thanks for your help. Right now I do have someone waiting. Please stay in close touch with me." Raul whispered, "Oh, and let's keep this between us. I don't think Captain McConnell needs to know that you're both going undercover," Raul winked.

"Raul, he'll never even know we were here," Ellen agreed. She gave Raul a quick hug and left his office.

She and Charlie started to walk towards the lobby when Ellen stopped and turned around abruptly. She was stunned to see Raul escorting someone familiar to his office. It was Sharon Thompson. "Hi, Sharon," Ellen called to her, puzzled.

"Oh, Ellen. It's you again," Sharon replied less than enthusiastically. Ellen waved as she and Charlie headed to the exit.

"Mrs. Thompson, please have a seat." Raul gestured to a chair and sat across from her at his desk. "I appreciate your being willing to come in to speak with me. Thank-you."

"I'm willing to do anything I can to help you find Cooper's murderer." Sharon looked so sincere, Raul thought she might begin to tear-up.

"That's reassuring. I was reviewing the conversation we had a couple of days after Cooper's murder and I just need to clarify a few things."

"Certainly, Detective." Sharon placed an elbow on the table and rested her chin in the palm of her hand.

"You said that you dropped off a check to Cooper at his apartment on Jackson Lane. How did you know his address?"

Sharon easily responded, "He asked everyone to feel free to send a donation to his Jackson Lane address. He posted it at every one of his concerts. We all knew about that sad little apartment, Detective Swann. He really deserved something so much nicer. Don't you agree?"

Raul smiled and continued. "Your donation was a very sizable one, Mrs. Thompson. You stated that your husband, Dr. Eli Thompson, was aware of this amount."

"That is correct. We don't keep secrets from one another."

Raul shook his head, "What continues to puzzle me is that when I asked Dr. Thompson about your donation, he was not at all happy about it."

Sharon was aghast to learn that Eli had been brought in for questioning. She pretended to casually laugh it off. "Well, Detective, while we don't keep secrets from each other, that doesn't mean we always agree on everything. I'm sure you understand that happens with couples."

Raul just stared at Sharon. Then, he continued, "Oh, and you told me that at the time of Cooper's murder, you were at home watching 'This is Us' on your iPad." Sharon nodded. Raul asked one more question. "Do you think Dr. Thompson would be able to verify your whereabouts?"

Sharon had had quite enough. "Detective, not only would Eli verify my whereabouts, but he would never let you get away with asking these offensive questions," she replied with indignation. "I am done here!" Sharon stood up and stormed out of Raul's office.

Raul knew that the Thompsons were both lying to him. Of that he was certain. However, he had no idea why. Neither one appeared to have a motive for killing Cooper.

Friday, March 15

"Bye, Charlie. See you later!" Ellen shouted as she raced out of the house. Catherine was honking the horn for her.

"Bye, Ellen! Have fun!"

Ellen climbed into the back seat. Karen, in the passenger seat, was amped up. "This will be a blast!"

Ignoring her comment, Catherine said, "Remember, we all told our husbands that we're going shopping, right?" Ellen and Karen nodded. "I can't believe I let you, two, talk me into this."

Karen reminded Catherine, "We really didn't, Catherine. All I know is that I saw this on Facebook and told you and Ellen about it. And, by the way, I'm glad to see that you got the memo about wearing black." Karen always prided herself on being dressed to the nines.

"Exactly my point. As soon as you told me that there was going to be a rally at the site of Cooper's murder, I couldn't let you go without me. You need me to babysit to make sure you, two, nutcases don't get in trouble!"

"Catherine, admit it. You didn't want to miss any of this!" Karen stated.

"That's ridiculous," Catherine denied. "This is a total waste of time. A bunch of old ladies like us are going to stand around staring at each other and wondering what the hell we're doing here. Besides, Cooper was a con man."

Ellen tried to put a different spin on this event. "But, Catherine, I'm going there undercover. I have a job to do, you know."

"Hah! Really, Ellen," was Catherine's response.

As they drove down El Dorado Parkway towards Crimson Court, they were shocked to see cars parked everywhere--on lawns, on sidewalks. They realized that they had better ditch Catherine's car as soon as possible. Catherine was less than thrilled about the questionable parking spot, but, then, she was less than thrilled about this entire expedition.

They followed the crowds and the noise, eventually arriving near the notorious poinciana tree where Cooper's body had been discovered. A veritable shrine had been created at the base of the tree. There was a guitar, bouquets of flowers, drawings, cards, signs, and even an old Beatle's album, "Rubber Soul", that featured Cooper's signature song, "Michelle".

However, even more impressive was the crowd. Women were all wearing black to show they were in mourning. Many carried placards saying things like "WE STILL LOVE YOU,COOPER", "AGE IS NOT A NUMBER", "I LEFT MY HUSBAND FOR YOU!", and "FIND THE KILLER NOW".

"If we get separated," Catherine yelled, "we'll meet up at Fathoms and wait for each other." Ellen and Karen nodded. Trying to be heard was hopeless. Ellen wriggled in closer to the shrine where the action was taking place. Karen and Catherine stayed close behind. Karen was chanting with the crowd, "FIND THE KILLER. FIND THE KILLER. FIND THE KILLER NOW!" Catherine held her phone above her head and randomly began taking videos. Local media was on the scene with reporters and cameras in motion. Catherine looked all around her and realized that the three of them were in the middle of this mob with swarms of women joining in from every direction. She found it disturbing that not one uniformed police officer was in sight.

Across the street, a counter protest made itself known. Men of the same vintage as the women began heckling the women, making sexist comments, howling, mocking them with cat-calls.

Without warning, Ellen, Karen, and Catherine were swept up in the Charge of the Light Brigade. They found themselves in the middle of a stampede, rushing towards the men. Karen held on to Ellen's hand to keep from getting trampled. Catherine stuck out her elbows to try to give herself some space. Ellen shrieked, "Hang on!" as she struggled to stay on her feet.

The angry mob of women in black began shaking their fists at the men. And, suddenly, this peaceful rally turned into a '60's feminist protest. As the mob lunged at the men, Ellen, Catherine, and Karen found themselves hurled to the frontline. Fearlessly, the women shouted, "SEXIST PIGS!" and "MURDERERS!" as they faced-off in a battle of the sexes. A couple of the women had worked themselves into a state of hysteria and began swatting at the men. Fortunately, their more sensible sisters were able to hold them back. For no apparent reason, women began dousing the men with water from their water bottles. The demonstration-gone-haywire looked like a geriatric version of the movie "Animal House".

Sirens blared as the Cape Coral Police Department, belatedly, arrived on the scene. The men backed off first and the women slowly retreated to their own side of the street. An ambulance parked itself in the middle of the street to provide any necessary medical attention. Scraped knees, bruises, and a few cases of dehydration were treated and released. Ellen, Catherine, and Karen decided to make their way to Fathoms for lunch despite their torn clothes and dripping wet hair. Their voices had completely disappeared from all their shouting.

Eli Thompson was not about to participate in the counter protest. However, he put on his binoculars and checked it out from afar. His hatred of Cooper had become an obsession. Therefore, he and his bruised ego sat in his car watching to see if his wife were stupid enough to be part of this crazy mob.

Catherine dropped Karen off at home first. Karen pulled her hat way down in an attempt to cover up her uncoiffed hair and tip-toed inside, hoping to slip by Bud. She was greatly relieved to see a note on the kitchen table, "Karen, went to pick up something to grill for dinner. Love, Bud."

Next, Catherine dropped Ellen off at home. Her shirt sleeve was badly ripped, the heel of her shoe had come off entirely, and her hair looked like a chia pet. She was trying to concoct a story as she opened the door. Fortunately, she was greeted by a note from Charlie: "Sweetie, went to play golf. Be back later. Love, Charlie."

Catherine was not the least bit worried about running into Ted. She knew how to shut him up. If he happened to be around, she would tell him the truth: "I was attacked by a mob of angry, old coots!" and just keep walking to the bathroom.

Saturday, March 16

Charlie got up early today and decided to walk to the beach before he and Ellen went to the Farmers' Market. He found it amusing that, by walking an hour earlier, he didn't see any of the usual walkers. So, he was caught off guard when Ted came up alongside him on his bicycle.

"Hey, Ted!"

"Charlie!" Ted got off his bicycle and walked along next to Charlie. "Not sure what's up, but I got a text from Bud this morning. He told me to find you and meet him at the Boat House."

"That's strange, but, sure. I'll be there in about fifteen minutes. See you then," Charlie said.

By the time Charlie arrived, Bud and Ted were already seated at a high-top table. Before Charlie could even say "hello", he was pre-empted by Bud who said evenly, "Look at this, Charlie," placing the Cape Coral Daily Breeze in front of him.

"What the hell is this!" Charlie was taken aback as he looked at the front-page photo. There was a large, color photo of yesterday's rally-turned-mêlée. And, front and center, were Ellen, Catherine, and Karen. Karen was caught leaning forward aggressively. Her mouth was wide open and she appeared to be shouting at a group of men. Ellen was in some guy's face screaming something, her hair dripping wet. And, Catherine was in the middle of heaving water from her

135

thermos at the mob of men. The headline read, "Geriatric Battle of the Sexes."

Bud read the entire article aloud while Charlie and Ted were aghast. Ted summed up the current state of affairs. "They told us they were going shopping and we fell for it."

Amy came over and took their coffee orders. "By the way, that was some brawl yesterday. Did you see the paper?"

Bud pointed to it on the table. "You mean this?" Amy burst into laughter and made a quick getaway.

"Okay, guys, so here's what we're going to do," Bud began, taking charge of the situation at hand. "Right now Karen has probably seen the paper and is panicking. She'll try to hide it from me."

"I'm sure Catherine will do the same," Ted concurred.

"So, we pretend we never saw the photo--that is, until dinner tonight. When we're at Merrick's, I'll just spread this out on the table and we'll go from there."

"Sounds good. In fact, why don't we suggest that they all wear the new outfits they, supposedly, bought yesterday?" Charlie added.

"Perfect!" Bud agreed.

When Amy brought their coffee, they checked out the photo once again. They totally lost it and began roaring with laughter, incapable of uttering a single, intelligible word.

Sharon poured her coffee and sat at the table on the lanai. She was fuming. Eli never told her he had been questioned. She was about to break their weeks of silence. "So, you were called in for questioning by Detective Swann and you never even told me about it!" she spewed.

Eli slowly looked up over his newspaper and calmly said, "Apparently, you must have been called in for questioning and, my dear, you never told me."

Ignoring his comment, Sharon continued, "You contradicted me and made me look foolish."

"Foolish or guilty?" Eli asked, looking straight at Sharon.

"You told him that you were angry with the donation I made to Cooper's fund."

"Sharon, let me put it this way. I wasn't angry. I was pissed!"

"Well, thanks, Eli. It makes me look guilty."

"Guilty of what? Being taken in by a con man?"

Sharon bristled at his comment. "And, I want to know what you told the detective about my alibi the night of the murder."

Eli shrugged his shoulders and said, "I told him I hadn't a clue where you were. We live very independent lives and don't pry into each other's business."

"You should have told me that you said all of this! I swore that you would be able to verify my whereabouts. Thanks, Eli. That makes me look like a liar."

"Perhaps. But, don't worry, Sharon. I have no intention of letting you look like a murderer. That wouldn't be good for either of us."

Eli looked back down at his paper. Sharon went inside to get ready for her facial scheduled for this morning.

By 7:00, Merrick's Fish Tale Grill was packed with a line going all the way to the sidewalk. This restaurant began as a fish market in 1991. By popular demand, the market expanded and opened up the Fish Tale Grill in 2013 so customers could enjoy fresh seafood while dining out. Merrick's loyal customers were always willing to wait, however, Catherine had somehow managed to reserve a table for six on the patio and they were seated fairly quickly. "So," Charlie said, "we guys were hoping to see the new outfits tonight."

Catherine retorted, "What I bought can only be seen by Ted. Sorry, boys."

"I have to have my skirt hemmed," Karen chimed in.

Ellen explained, "I saved you a fortune yesterday, Sweetie. Couldn't find a thing!"

Bud looked somber as he asked, "Did you hear about the Cooper rally yesterday?" Wide-eyed looks of innocence passed from Ellen to Catherine to Karen.

"No, dear," Karen said. "What happened?"

The server handed each of them a menu before Bud could reply. They paused to look over the menu.

Bud continued, "Well, it seems that a crowd of women gathered to pay homage to this guy Cooper. I don't get it, but that's what they were doing. And, then, a group of men gathered in protest."

"Really?" Ellen exclaimed in surprise.

Catherine asked warily, "Bud, how did you hear about this?"

"Everyone at the Boat House was amped up about it."

"So, dear," Karen smiled sweetly, "what happened?"

"It became a real brawl and the police had to break it up. What do you think about that?"

Before anyone could respond, the server returned to take their orders. "I heard you talking about the rally yesterday. That was totally crazy! My neighbor went and she said the police had to use a bullhorn to be heard. And, the women were more hostile than the men. Can you believe it?" she sighed. "So, what'll you have?" The server turned to Ellen first.

"I'll have the bourbon salmon and, by the way, the men were more hostile than the women," Ellen snipped. "But, of course, how would I know?" she quickly backpedaled.

After everyone ordered, Bud triumphantly plunked the newspaper on the table. The three men folded their arms and looked at their wives, waiting for an explanation.

Catherine kept her cool. She slowly put on her glasses, stared at the photo, looked up and said, "Isn't that funny? Those women in the front almost look like us!" She practically hyperventilated trying to stifle a laugh.

Within seconds, they were all well past the point of no return, and, control was no longer an option. The six of them threw back their heads and, simply, howled with laughter.

Sunday, March 17

Ellen was half-asleep when her phone rang. She saw that it was Beverly, so she grudgingly answered it. "Yes, Beverly?"

"And, my daughter wants *you* to check up on *me*? Hah! That's a joke."

"What are you talking about, Beverly? It's 7:30 in the morning. This better be important."

"Well, I am looking at a photo of you in yesterday's paper, Ellen, and," Beverly paused to compose herself, "you really need to do something about that hair!" she cackled.

"Yeah, thanks a lot, Beverly."

"No problem, dear. But, I will make sure to check up on you soon. I do think you're going a bit batty. I have to go! I have a tennis match this morning."

Ellen gritted her teeth and thought to herself, "I hope she double faults!"

Charlie had plans to play golf. Paul Shapiro had arranged a foursome. Stan, one of the golfers who lived nearby, just pulled into the driveway. Charlie grabbed his clubs and said good-bye to Ellen.

After their round of golf, the foursome headed to the bar on the patio of the clubhouse to have a couple of beers. There was the usual ribbing about missed putts and balls landing in the water hazards. Charlie and Paul had to endure their opponents bragging about their winning birdies on the eighteenth hole. Then, they each introduced themselves to another foursome seated nearby.

It was only a matter of time before someone brought up the Cooper rally. "And, did you see the photo in the Breeze?" one of the guys laughed.

"Yeah. I wouldn't want to mess with any of those babes!" another guy piped up.

"Definitely not my type," Shapiro chuckled. "Actually," he leaned in and whispered, "I was called in to the police station for questioning on Friday." That comment got everyone's full attention. Paul seemed to relish the moment. "The police were checking up on every phone contact, so I was told to show up. Cooper was one of my patients, you know. Even had to cancel an expensive crown, damnit!" A loud round of guffaws followed.

"So what did they ask you?"

"I guess, the usual stuff: what was Cooper like, did he floss regularly?" Another round of laughs. Clearly, Shapiro delighted in entertaining his audience.

Someone else asked, "Do the police have a suspect?"

"Who knows. But, I'll bet it's some jealous husband, if you ask me," another guy conjectured.

A doughy golfer seated at the opposite end of the bar chimed in, "Hah! That's hard to imagine! Did you get a good look at that pack of crazy women?"

The two foursomes bantered on about the rally. Charlie remained unusually silent, preferring to focus his attention on his beer.

Sunday was family day at the Yacht Club beach. Toddlers were squealing and running into the water, terrifying their grandparents. Teenage girls were working on their tans and pretending not to notice the teenage boys who were gaping at them. Parents were shlepping sunscreen, food, towels, beach tents, and beach chairs with pull-out food trays. They appeared to be settling in until the onset of hurricane season.

Ellen, eventually, found a parking place near the racquetball courts and walked to the beach, carrying her New York Times, a beach chair, and her purse. She found a semi-shaded place on the beach and made herself comfortable. After an hour or so, Ellen became frustrated trying to figure out the theme of the crossword puzzle. She picked up her purse and walked to the Boat House to get a cold drink. Stella was sitting next to the railing overlooking the beach. She was sipping a Boat House Bloody Mary. Ellen walked over to say hello.

"Hi, Stella. Not sure if you remember me. I'm Ellen Green." Stella looked at Ellen quizzically. Ellen added, "You probably remember my husband, Charlie. Big guy. Very friendly. We met one morning right here."

143

"Yes, now that you mention it, I do remember him. 'Ellen' you say your name is? Ellen?" Stella mused. "Now I remember our conversation." Stella eyed Ellen suspiciously. "It was right after Cooper's murder. I told you about my neighbor, Mildred, and her will, didn't I?"

Ellen nodded. She had an uneasy feeling that this conversation was quickly heading downhill. "That's right."

"And, I remember that I told you to keep quiet about it, didn't I?" Ellen nodded again, sheepishly. "Well, Frank Blake paid me a visit the other day. He was livid. He said that some good friend of mine, named Ellen, stopped by!" Stella's voice could be heard above the racket of the Boat House crowd. She was becoming increasingly agitated.

"What else did he say?" Ellen was trying to figure out how to diffuse Stella's anger.

Stella glared at Ellen as she said, "Frank was furious with me and accused me of telling you about his mother's will. I denied it and told him I didn't know anyone named Ellen. Actually, I had no idea, until this moment, that he was right. I had no clue who this 'Ellen' person was until now." Stella continued to glare at Ellen. "And, I don't know why I ever told you about Mildred's will in the first place."

"Stella, I never said a word to Frank about Mildred's will. Please believe me," Ellen pleaded.

"What the hell were you doing at his place, asking questions?"

"You're right. I had no business going to see Frank. I am, truly, sorry, Stella." Ellen wasn't the least bit sorry, but she knew she had to kiss up or butt out. She opted for kissing up. "But, Stella, if he was so paranoid, I'd have to wonder why. Wouldn't you?"

Stella softened and nodded in agreement. "He got in my face and told me that this was none of my business."

"He threatened you?" Ellen was stunned.

"Well, nothing specific, but I was, and still am, shaken by his behavior," Stella admitted.

"Stella, the police need to know about this." Ellen wrote the name of Detective Sergeant Raul Swann on a napkin. "You need to ask for Detective Swann. He's a friend of mine and you can trust him, Stella." Before handing her the napkin, Ellen added her own name and phone number. "Please contact the police about Frank. And, know that you can always call me--anytime."

"No way! I'm sorry, Ellen, but I need to go now," Stella stated as she paid her check. "I'm not easily scared off, but I really think Frank Blake would kill me if he ever found out I went to the police."

Ellen and Stella locked eyes as the same disturbing revelation hit them both.

The warm, sunny afternoon boded well for another magnificent sunset. Therefore, Ellen and Charlie decided to enjoy it from the new Boat House Tiki Bar that recently opened up in Fort Myers. This second location is a more expansive version of the Cape Coral location with outdoor dining, a fire pit, and, even a swimming pool for customers! However, the same menu, upbeat staff, and Caribbean feel abound. Ellen and Charlie were escorted to a table alongside the Caloosahatchee. They were grooving to the live music and drinking their margaritas when Ellen looked over and saw an all-too familiar face several tables from her: Beverly Miller.

"Psst, Charlie. That's Beverly whose daughter keeps wanting me to check on her," Ellen whispered, gesturing with her head.

"Oh. Well, why don't you go over and say 'hello' to her?"

"Charlie, she's already enjoyed humiliating me once today. I'm not going to subject myself to her snide comments again!"

Charlie looked over and saw that Beverly was approaching their table. "Ellen, you may not have a choice," he warned.

"Ellen, what a surprise! And who is this handsome young man you're with?" Beverly asked coyly.

"Oh, Beverly, hi! Beverly Miller, my husband, Charlie."

"Pleased to meet you, Beverly." Charlie rose and shook Beverly's hand, thoroughly amused by Ellen's reaction.

"Charlie, delighted," Beverly replied. "Hope you can keep Ellen's picture out of the newspaper for a while. She makes all of us mature women look rather silly, I'm afraid," Beverly chided. "Anyhow, enjoy your evening."

146

"You, too, Beverly. Good to see you again," Ellen grimaced.

Captain McConnell had summoned Detective Swann for a meeting. McConnell began, "Swann, we seem to be getting nowhere with this Cooper investigation. We've gotten names but nothing concrete in terms of a possible motive. The Chief is starting to put pressure on the department. If he follows through with his threat to get the State involved, we're going to look like bumbling idiots!"

"Sir, I'll do whatever I can to move this along. You have my word."

"Well, move it along now! I don't know how much longer I can hold off the Chief."

Raul nodded, "Yes, Sir. I'll keep you posted."

Raul returned to his office. Ellen and Charlie Green were due to arrive any minute. He was hopeful that the Greens had a lead for him. "Yes, Sergeant Drake. Please show them in."

"Hi Ellen, Charlie."

"Hello Raul."

"Please sit down. You said that you had some information."

Ellen told Raul about the meeting with Mildred's son, Frank Blake. Next, she recapped her meeting with Stella.

"So, Stella is afraid to tell us that Frank Blake threatened her?" Raul summed up.

"That's right. I pleaded with her to contact you, but she won't. You're going to have to contact her."

"You realize, Ellen, that when I come knocking on her door to question her, she'll know you gave me this information."

"Well, I never promised that *I* wouldn't get in touch with you," Ellen said shrewdly. "Anyhow, I have no idea of Stella's address or last name."

Raul smiled, "Ellen, I admit, we haven't, yet, found the murderer, but we are quite capable of locating Stella. I assure you."

"Now, if you need our help, which, clearly, you do, you need to share some of your leads," Ellen asserted.

Raul nodded in agreement. "Here's what we have." He pulled out a chart with names, circles, arrows, lines, and dotted lines. Cooper, A.K.A. Mark Simmons, was in a circle in the middle of the chart. "There's Maya Wolfson. She's been lying to us. We already know that she was in his penthouse between Saturday, February 23 and Tuesday, February 26." Ellen and Charlie looked surprised by this finding. "And, through you, we know that she has a possible motive if she thought that Cooper was going to steal her songs. Did she know about his recording deal? We're pretty sure that she did. In fact, her fingerprints were found on his computer. Alibi? None."

Ellen and Charlie waited for Raul to continue. "Ned Abbott. He was a contact on Cooper's phone. He lives in El Paso and knew Cooper and Maya when they were in Austin, years ago. Maya swears that Abbott was the songwriter, not her. I think they've been in touch

149

with each other. We're finding that out right now--checking their mobile phone records. Maya and Ned are, both, persons of interest."

Next, Raul pointed to Sharon Thompson. "She's been a very generous donor to the bogus senior music studio fund. Seemed to be a devoted fan and was in frequent contact with Cooper for months. She's holding out about something, but I don't know what. At this point, I can't come up with a strong motive. Then, there's her husband, Dr. Eli Thompson. He seemed enraged about his wife's donations, but is that a reason to murder Cooper? Doesn't add up."

Ellen looked perplexed. "Raul, you said that Sharon Thompson was a devoted fan?" Raul nodded. "She hated Cooper! She talked about how most women fell for his act, but she didn't."

"You know her?" Raul asked. "How did you meet Sharon Thompson?"

"Raul, you really don't want to hear that story. Believe me!" Charlie chimed in. "Does Sharon know that you spoke with her husband?"

"She sure knows that, now that I told her. But she pretended that they share everything with each other. It was a desperate cover-up for something. I can't figure out why she would pretend to like Cooper if she really despised him," Raul mused. "So we're left with Sharon Thompson. No apparent motive at this time. Alibi was weak."

"And, there's Dr. Eli Thompson," Ellen reminded them. "Both of them seem sketchy to me."

Charlie was mulling over this information. "Maybe it was a crime of passion."

"What do you mean, Charlie?" Raul asked.

"What if Sharon Thompson thought she and Cooper were in love and discovered that, instead, he had used her for her money. The woman scorned, so to speak."

"It's possible, Charlie, but Mrs. Thompson struck me as much too calculating to fall for Cooper."

Ellen scoffed, "Raul, that's why you need us. You're thinking the way a young detective would think. You don't have any idea what's it's like to feel old and unattractive. Cooper made women of my age feel sexy. That was his gift."

"Go on," Raul encouraged her.

"Well," Ellen concluded, "I think it's pretty clear. You need me to get Sharon drunk so I can learn what she's hiding."

"Sounds like a plan," Raul agreed.

Charlie added, "And, you need me to talk to Maya to get more info from her."

Ellen agreed. "Maya seemed to have a soft spot for Charlie. He'll get her to talk."

"Alright. Let's see where we are," Raul got out a pen and pad of paper. "Ellen, you're going to follow up with Sharon. Charlie, you're

151

going to speak with Maya. I'll follow up with Stella and with Frank Blake. The department will have more data about Ned Abbott today." Raul paused to look at Ellen and Charlie. "And, we meet back here on Wednesday."

"Bye, Raul. See you Wednesday." Ellen and Charlie were ready to get to work on their assignments.

Seconds later there was a knock on Raul's office door. "Come on in!"

Captain McConnell stood scratching his head. "Did I just see the Greens come out of your office?"

"Yes, Sir," Raul said, clearing his throat.

"Should I be concerned about this?"

"Not at all," Raul smiled. "They stopped by to congratulate me. They had heard that Jennifer and I are going to have a baby."

"Okay, Raul. Yes, and, er, congratulations," McConnell said awkwardly.

"Thanks, Sir. Have a good day."

On the drive home, Charlie couldn't help but wonder how Ellen expected Sharon to agree to meet with her. "Ellen, you two haven't exactly hit it off, you know," he stated carefully.

"You're right, Charlie, but I'll come up with something." Ellen was in a pickle and she knew it. They rode home in silence, each pondering their own mission.

A detour to Paesano's Italian Market was the distraction Ellen and Charlie, each, needed to clear their heads. As they entered the market, they were greeted with a rich tenor voice belting out "O Sole Mio" from the speakers. Instead of thinking about sleuthing, they filled their heads with the sounds and smells of old world Italy. Rose, the owner, recommended an imported hard cheese and the olive mix. They took her advice and headed home to Wisteria Court.

Maybe it was the earthy flavor of the cheese or maybe it was the zesty olives. Regardless, as soon Ellen finished eating, she blurted out, "I've got it, Charlie."

"What have you got?"

"I know how I can get together with Sharon: Pamela Green!"

"Okay, tell me."

"Charlie, I don't have time to tell you. I've got to call Pamela up right now." Ron and Pamela Green had come to their rescue last year. Ellen was sure Pamela wouldn't let her down. Ellen called and left a message. Pamela called right back and Ellen explained this dicey situation.

"So, you think Sharon could have murdered Cooper?" Pamela was shocked.

"No idea, Pamela. But, we do know that Sharon has been lying to Detective Swann. So, I agreed to try to find out what she's covering up."

"Well, let me see. I'll invite her for a drink. Sharon would never turn down a good, dry martini. Let's make it tomorrow afternoon at 3:00."

"Pamela, you're the best! Thanks."

"I'm looking forward to it. See you tomorrow. Nauti-Mermaid."

"But, how will you explain me?" Ellen asked.

Pamela began laughing, "Ellen, to quote Charlie: 'I'm not even going to try!'"

Raul wasn't keen on calling Beverly Miller, but he had to corroborate two statements that Ellen made. One, did Beverly actually hear Cooper say he had signed a recording deal? And, two, did Cooper tell her that he was going to record an album of his original songs? He called Beverly's number.

"Yes, Detective Swann. So nice to hear from you. It has been a while since you cancelled our last meeting."

"Yes, Beverly. I was sorry to have to cancel. How have you been?"

"Busy. And you?" Beverly asked with an edge to her voice.

"Busy. Beverly, I wondered if I could stop by tomorrow afternoon. I'd like to ask you a few more questions about your conversation with Cooper."

"Detective, I would love to help out, but Tuesday is not possible. I have a tennis match tomorrow and I wouldn't feel right skipping it. I'd be letting my team down. Sorry."

"Well, perhaps we could do this over the phone," Raul suggested.

"As long as you make it quick, Detective. As I said earlier, I am a very busy person."

"Beverly, I appreciate your taking the time to help me. And, once again, I really do need your assistance. I wouldn't bother you if it weren't very important." Raul knew how to play her game.

"Alright. In that case, what questions do you have, Detective?"

"Two questions. Did Cooper tell you he had signed a recording deal?"

"Oh, yes. He was very excited about it but wanted to keep it hush-hush."

"And, Beverly, did he describe the album to you?"

"He certainly did. It was going to be entirely his original songs. Imagine that!"

"Thank-you, Beverly. You've been extremely helpful."

155

"Any time, Detective Swann. Well, as long as I don't have a tennis match," she chuckled. "Gotta run!"

"Good-bye, Beverly."

That evening at Maria's, Charlie was grateful that there was no talk of Cooper or rallies or sleuthing. They all appeared to be six, typical retirees in their seventies enjoying half-price pizza night together, well, at least, until Ellen casually inquired about whether Sharon had been going to water aerobics lately.

Karen couldn't wait to fill her in. "Funny you should ask. She sashayed in today and made sure to let us all know that she wouldn't be showing up tomorrow."

"As if any of us cared," Catherine interjected. "We were too busy gasping for breath, trying to do our leg lifts in the deep end."

"But, it was obvious, she hoped someone would ask her why she wasn't coming to class on Tuesday."

"And, we were all too stubborn to ask her," Catherine gave Karen a look of annoyance, "until you couldn't hold out any longer. Isn't that right, Karen?"

"Look, I was proud of myself for resisting as long as I did!" Karen admitted.

"So, Karen, what did she say?" Ellen asked nonchalantly.

156

"She bragged about being invited for a drink by Pamela Green. You know, Ellen, your friend. She made sure to tell us that Pamela owns the Cape Coral Resort at la-di-da village."

"Whatever," Catherine muttered.

"Well, that's quite the invite!" Ellen exclaimed. She and Charlie exchanged a quick glance.

Tuesday, March 19

Ned Abbott groaned when he saw it was 6:30 A.M. He answered his phone, "Maya, do you realize what time it is here in El Paso?"

"And, do you realize I've been trying to get in touch with you for days now, but you're ignoring my calls?" Maya snapped. "Listen to me, Ned. The police have questioned me and they know I've lied to them. What the hell am I supposed to tell them?"

"Okay, okay. Calm down, Maya. I'll think of something." He rolled over and went back to sleep.

Ellen showed up at Nauti-Mermaid promptly at 3:00. Pamela was waiting for her at a table shaded by an umbrella in the shape of a yellow sail. Unlike their husbands, who fully prescribed to the "wing-it" method, Pamela and Ellen strategized in preparation for Sharon's arrival. The plan was pretty basic: get Sharon soused. They gleefully toasted each other with their virgin gin and tonics.

Twenty minutes later, Sharon waved as she approached Pamela's table. "Yoo-hoo!"

"Sharon, so good to see you." As they hugged, Sharon glanced over at Ellen. "What a surprise, Ellen."

"Hi, Sharon! We meet again," she said cheerily.

"So, what brings you here?" Sharon asked guardedly.

158

Pamela jumped right in. "Ellen had stopped by to purchase a gift certificate. I flagged her down and asked her to join us for a drink. Todd," she called to the server, "we'd like to order some drinks."

"Sure, Mrs. Green. Ladies, what can I get for you?"

"I'd like a gin and tonic, please," Ellen said.

"And, I'll have a dry martini, up, with a lemon," Sharon said.

"And, a gin and tonic for me," Pamela said with a smile.

Todd gave her a knowing wink and promptly returned with the drinks. Pamela had prepped him, in advance, on the importance of momentum to this operation. The conversation flowed effortlessly with Pamela taking the lead. She asked Ellen about what she and Charlie had been up to. Next, she asked Sharon about her recent trip to Virgin Gorda.

While Sharon was chattering away about her Caribbean cruise, Pamela signaled to Todd, pointing to Sharon's martini glass. He returned and, swiftly, exchanged Sharon's empty glass for a full one. As anticipated, by the third martini, Sharon's tempo increased. Sips turned to swallows. Swallows turned into slurps. Slurps turned into gulps.

"So, what do you think about that crazy Cooper rally on Friday?" Pamela decided that the time for action had arrived.

Ellen hoped that a modest confession might facilitate an exchange of confidences. "I must admit, it was fun."

159

"You were there?" Sharon asked. "Ellen, I didn't think you'd be infatuated with that phony!"

Ellen shrugged, "He was so cute. It was hard not to be, don't you agree?"

"Are you kidding! He stole money from all of those women. Say, Pamela, could we get something to snack on? I don't like drinking on an empty stomach."

"Sure, Sharon. Todd?"

Todd miraculously appeared on cue. "Yes, Mrs. Green?"

"A platter of crudités and another round of drinks, please."

"Coming right up," he announced.

"You were saying that Cooper stole money from the women," Pamela reminded Sharon. "But, you gave him a lot of money, too. I remember you talked about it."

"Hah! A pittance compared to the others. Believe me!" Sharon paused to finish her third martini before continuing. "But, I gave him something that the other old cows didn't!" She leaned in close to Ellen and Pamela with a gleam in her eye. "A kick in the butt!" she brayed.

Pamela's perplexed expression was all the encouragement that Sharon needed. "Did you know that Cooper and I met for private luncheons and afternoon drinks?" she whispered secretly.

Ellen thought to herself, "Everyone knew about this." Aloud, she asked, "Sharon, you gave Cooper 'a kick in the butt'?"

Sharon leaned forward on her forearms and confessed, "Actually, I lied." She went on, "He gave me the kick in the butt: the creep dumped me."

Ellen and Pamela cried in unison, "No way!"

Sharon nodded, "And, yes, I did contribute to his senior bullshit fund." Todd arrived with a platter and a fresh round of drinks. Sharon bit into a carrot and continued, "Eli was absolutely livid! Livid!"

"Was he jealous?" Pamela asked.

"Eli, jealous?" Sharon waved the carrot around in tandem with her head shaking. "Pfft. You must be kidding. The only thing Eli cares about is money. Well, money and his precious reputation."

"What do you mean about Cooper dumping you?" Ellen asked.

Sharon took a gulp of martini number four and slurred, "I gave Coop what 'e wanned and 'e dumped me!" Sharon's eyes filled with tears, smearing her mascara.

Pamela and Ellen braced themselves, expecting graphic details of Sharon and Cooper's sexual exploits. But, instead, Sharon blurted out, "MONEY! It was all about money to Coop."

"Did you..."

161

Oblivious to everyone around her, Sharon interrupted, "He used me and I really, really, REALLY," she paused, momentarily forgetting what it was she wanted to say, "loved him." Sharon sobbed.

Pamela gave her a napkin to wipe her eyes. Sharon dabbed and, then, dipped a red pepper in the remoulade sauce. She stopped bawling as suddenly as she began. In fact, she sounded unnaturally calm and sober. "I hated the bastard. Passionately hated him," she stated icily.

"You hated him?" Ellen pretended to be shocked.

Sharon nodded and honked noisily as she blew her nose. "Hey, hey! Another martini. Over here!" She rudely flagged down Todd, holding her empty glass above her head.

She leaned in towards Ellen and Pamela and, furtively, announced, "You know, it all started about a month ago. He kept making excuses and breaking our dates. So, I began stalking him to see who he dumped me for." She put her finger in front of her mouth and spoke in a low voice. "I think it was some rich bitch who lived in those condos on Crimson Court. Every night, I'd see him walk to the same fancy-shmancy building and he never knew I was there."

Ellen didn't dare to breathe for fear of dousing this verbal combustion. Pamela was silent. Sharon reprimanded Todd, "It's about time!" She took a slurp of her drink, and continued to spew. "I wanna know who this slut was who took Coop away from me!" Her eyes narrowed, menacingly.

"Did you follow him on the night he was murdered?" Ellen brashly asked.

162

"Well, let's see now. Maybe I did and, then, again, maybe I didn't," she replied coquettishly. "Look, you, two, he got what he deserved." Sharon leaned on one elbow to keep herself upright. Holding her glass in front of her, she toasted, "Here's to Cooper's killer. May she be ever victorious!"

Sharon took one last swig of her drink and face-planted smack into the remoulade. Ellen and Pamela cleaned her off. With one of them on each side, they were, eventually, able to maneuver Sharon into Ellen's van. Ellen strapped her in, blasted the air-conditioning in Sharon's face, and drove away.

On the ride home, Ellen attempted to extract whatever information she could from Sharon. "Sharon, did you ever see him with anyone or was he always alone?"

Sharon babbled, "I didn't need to see him with anyone to know he dumped me for some rich, ole fart. That's for damn sure! But, oh, yeah, very late one night, I saw him with some young chickie. And, it was disgusting. They were clutching and grabbing at each other like a couple of animals in heat. Disgusting!"

"When was that?"

"Hell--I don't remember but it was in front of some apartment on..."

"Yes? Where was it, Sharon?"

"You really think I could remember that?" Sharon scoffed. "It was on..." Sharon looked befuddled.

"Try to think, Sharon!"

"Santa Barbara! Yes, that's it," Sharon exclaimed in relief, as if that recollection proved she wasn't blotto.

Ellen parked in Sharon's driveway and helped Sharon to the front door. They staggered in and stood face-to-face with Eli glaring down at them. Ellen broke the silence, "She's a bit tipsy, I'm afraid."

"Is she? Well, what a surprise," he said sarcastically. "Sharon, just sit down here." Eli helped her to the couch. "Thank-you for bringing her home. I'll take over now." He shook Ellen's hand and escorted her to the door.

Ellen stood outside the door and listened. She was richly rewarded. "You're drunk!"

"Ooh, you noticed! And, guess what, Eli, for once, I didn't care what I said. In fact, Eli, dear, it's possible--just a teensy bit possible--that I said some things I shouldn't have!" Sharon giggled uncontrollably.

"What the hell were you thinking!" Eli yelled.

"I wasn't. I wasn't thinking at all. And guess what, I don't remember what I said," Sharon tittered.

Ellen knew she better take off before she got caught snooping. Therefore, she never heard what happened next. Eli grabbed Sharon by the shoulders and snarled, "Well, you better start remembering what you said or you could be spending the rest of your life in an orange jumpsuit!"

With all her might, Sharon whipped the back of her hand right across Eli's arrogant face.

Charlie had no chance to speak with Ellen when she returned home. As soon as she pulled into the driveway and got out, Charlie climbed into the van and drove off. He was trying to track down Maya. Fortunately, Ellen had written down the gigs that Maya mentioned when they had lunch at Matlacha. So, he was confident that Maya would be setting up the sound for the jazz ensemble scheduled to appear at Slate's this evening. She was finishing up her last sound check when she spotted Charlie.

"Hi, Charlie! Nice to see you."

"You, too, Maya. You're busy this evening, I see."

"Was busy," she replied. "But, now everything's all set. You in a hurry?"

"Not at all. Let me buy you a drink."

"Sure! Bob, I'd like my usual and a half-dozen raw oysters. Charlie's paying."

Bob raised his eyebrows and grinned at Charlie. "Here you go, Maya," Bob said, handing her a draft of Abita Amber. "Charlie?"

"A Stella, Bob. By the way, Ellen and I really liked your song, the other day," Charlie said.

"Thanks. It was fun to try it out in front of an audience."

"You thinking of starting to spend more time on your songwriting?"

165

"Like I said, my first priority is making money from sound jobs," Maya explained. "But, I always find time to write."

"With all your contacts, Maya, you could probably get a recording deal."

"It's never that simple. It's a cut-throat business," she answered, taking a swig of her beer.

"Really?"

"Oh, yes. If you're a nobody like me, it doesn't matter how good your songs are. The record labels don't want to risk it, so they'll stick to big names or some up-and-coming, hot, new singer."

"Like Cooper?"

Maya nodded. "That's right. Cooper already had a following, so any record label is guaranteed solid sales."

"Bob, another round for Maya and me, please." Charlie continued, "But, you said he never wrote a single song."

Maya looked up at Charlie. "The most celebrated artists are notorious for stealing from other artists. Brian Wilson's "Surfin' U.S.A." was stolen from Chuck Berry. Even the Beatles were sued for stealing."

Charlie asked, "So, what does this have to do with Cooper?"

"You think he was any better than the others?"

"What do you mean?"

166

"Charlie, Cooper was a fraud in every way!" Maya became incensed. "He used people to get whatever he wanted from them."

"So, you think he used you, too?"

Maya clenched her jaw as her eyes narrowed. "I know he did."

"What makes you say that?"

"Charlie, I really shouldn't be talking about any of this with you." Maya turned her attention to an oyster and let it slither down her throat.

"Maya, you have a talent and you need to do what you can to protect your songs or somebody else will end up getting rich on your creativity," Charlie said.

"Look, Charlie, stop treating me like I'm some innocent waif. Believe me, I know how to handle the Coopers in this world! And, a whole lot better than you do!" she snapped. "The bastard actually tried to buy my collection of songs but I refused to sell them."

"Why did you refuse? You've talked about needing the money."

"Charlie, what he offered me was insulting. But, it's much more complicated than that."

"What do you mean?"

"Do you really want to hear this?" Charlie nodded and Maya continued. "Okay." She sighed, "Back about ten years ago, I ended up in Austin. That's where I met Cooper and his buddy, Ned. We

167

met at a bar and started jamming together. I was into writing songs and, before I knew it, Ned and I were collaborating. We wrote some damn, good stuff together. A couple of years later, we all went our separate ways, but Ned and I continued to stay in touch and we kept on writing songs together."

"So, did you try to record them?"

"Nah. We were too busy doing what we needed to do to pay our bills. But Cooper had only one talent to fall back on," Maya said with disgust as she downed another oyster. "He discovered that his real gift wasn't his voice. It was his ability to cheat."

Charlie cocked his head. "Cheat?"

"Look, we know he conned all those women and, then, he thought he could con me."

"So, what happened when you refused his offer?"

"He gave me his smarmy smile and said that he was only trying to help me out." Maya began to raise her voice as she became agitated. "What bullshit that was! I knew he was ruthless and would do whatever it took to get what he wanted. What he didn't realize was that I was just as ruthless and, even worse, I was onto him!" Maya spewed. "And, this time, I was the one with all the power, not him!"

"Yes?"

"What I knew about him could destroy him," she uttered with venom. "Let me just say that I knew a whole lot about Cooper and his phony life-style, his phony music fund. His art was that he knew how to scam everyone."

"Why was he so determined to steal your songs? He already had fans screaming for him when he sang. He didn't need your songs."

"There was something else, too. Charlie, this stays between us," Maya suddenly leaned towards him and whispered. "A few weeks ago, Ned called me to warn me that Cooper had just signed a record deal. He was going to produce an album of his original songs."

"A record deal? And you heard it from Ned, not from Cooper?"

"Exactly," Maya sneered.

"Funny, he mentioned it to his friend, but not to you," Charlie said.

"Yeah, isn't it, Charlie?" Maya replied with feigned surprise. "And his original songs? Really?"

"Did Cooper know that you were aware of his record deal?"

Before Maya could answer, a lanky man, around fifty, slid onto the stool next to her. He turned to face her and asked, "Hey, Babe, don't I even get a hug from you these days?" He slowly stood next to her.

Maya looked aghast. The stranger scooped her into his arms in a big bear hug. Charlie rose to his feet and glowered at the guy, ready to mix it up. The stranger let Maya go. When she landed, she said, her voice quivering, "Charlie, meet Ned Abbott."

Charlie's firm, unyielding grip was more of a warning rather than a greeting. Both men stared each other down. Maya broke the stand-off. "What are you doing here?"

"Thought I'd take a vacation for a couple of weeks. Wanted to surprise you, Maya. It's been quite a while, hasn't it?" Ned taunted. "Ya know," he winked, "gotta keep an eye on this one. She can be pretty slippery." He banged his fist on the bar trying to get Bob's attention. "Hey, dude. A beer!"

The music from the jazz ensemble, playing in the other room, was piped into the bar. Bob discreetly amped up the volume so the other customers couldn't hear the heated exchange he knew was about to take place. Bob ignored him and sauntered over when he was good and ready. "Yeah. What'll it be?"

"Whatever Grandpa's drinking," Ned said pointing to Charlie's glass. Bob poured him a Stella and plunked it down hard. "So, Charlie, I came all the way from El Paso to clean up a bit of a mess around here. Maya's mess."

"Shut up, Ned!" Maya spit out.

"Poor, Maya! I was far away in El Paso when Cooper got bumped off. But, Maya, where were you?" He leaned on the bar in Charlie's direction as he mocked her. "Aw, now, see Charlie, Maya has quite a temper when you call her out. Right, Maya?"

Maya was seething with rage but just stared down at her beer. Ned continued to provoke her. "Doesn't look good for Maya that she confronted Cooper about stealing our songs and, boom, a couple of days later he's dead!"

"Then, tell me, what the hell are you doing here?" Charlie asked angrily.

Ned splayed out his hands and innocently pleaded, "I'm here to rescue the damsel in distress. Maya called and Ned came running."

"You bastard!" Maya grumbled. "Hah! You're the last person I want to see."

Charlie had had enough. He stood up and loomed, menacingly, over Ned. "You better behave like a perfect gentleman. I've had it with you and your bullying." Turning to Maya, Charlie scribbled out his phone number and said, "Take this. If this piece of crap gives you any more trouble, call me!"

Maya grabbed the paper and yelled back, "I don't need your help! Why don't you, both, just leave me alone!" She stormed out and slammed the door.

Charlie and Ned sat silently. Bob looked straight at Ned and growled under his breath, "You can take your sorry ass right back to El Paso. Don't you dare come in here, ever again."

Ned gulped down his beer. Charlie put money down on the bar and said to Bob, "This should cover everything, Bob. I'll take care of junior, over here, too." Charlie shot Ned a withering look and walked out the door.

Ellen and Charlie were, each, drained from a grueling day. In fact, as they climbed into the hot tub, neither one wanted to relive their exhausting experiences. Charlie suggested they relax, with a glass of wine, in total silence. They could talk when they met with Raul the next day at the police station. To his astonishment, Ellen agreed wholeheartedly. They welcomed the quiet. The only sound to be heard was the rush of water from the jets--and an occasional "aah".

Wednesday, March 20

This morning, Detective Sergeant Raul Swann had one more stop to make before returning to the police station. He rang the doorbell of an attractive home on Mangrove Court. A woman cautiously asked, "Who is it?"

"Stella Reynolds, I'm Detective Sergeant Swann. I'd like a word with you, please."

"Can you hold up some I.D.?" Raul complied and the door opened a crack.

"May I come in?"

Stella eyed him suspiciously as she invited him into the living room. They shook hands and Raul explained, "It has come to my attention that Frank Blake, your neighbor's son, has threatened you."

"Well, not exactly threatened," Stella replied. "He was overwrought and took it out on me."

Raul nodded and explained, "Mrs. Reynolds, I have spoken with Mr. Blake and I don't think he'll bother you again."

Stella said uneasily, "I hope he didn't think I put you up to this."

Raul smiled, "Don't worry. But, if he contacts you, you need to call me at once. Here's my card."

Stella took the card and looked at Raul quizzically. "It was that Ellen woman who told you, wasn't it?"

"Mrs. Reynolds, our department is investigating every possible contact that Cooper had. That includes following up on every, single person who donated to his fund--even the ones who are deceased."

Stella seemed somewhat reassured. "Thank-you, Detective. Good-day."

"Good-day, Mrs. Reynolds."

Raul got back into his car and thought about his visit to Frank Blake yesterday. He had, vehemently, denied every accusation Raul threw at him. Blake played the devoted, grieving son who was very grateful to Stella for driving Mildred wherever she wanted to go. And, yes, of course, Mildred was a big Cooper fan. Frank said, "Cooper was like a second son to my mother." Raul didn't buy this show of generosity, but, for now, a warning seemed to get him to back off and leave Stella alone.

Ellen and Charlie arrived at the Cape Coral Police Department to meet with Raul. They had information to share. Raul asked Charlie to start filling them in. Charlie began, "Look, what I do know is that Cooper tried to buy Maya's original songs and she refused his offer. According to Maya, he offered her almost nothing for them. She was well aware that Cooper was a con man. She didn't trust him and seemed to have a real chip on her shoulder."

Raul asked, "Did she know about his record deal?"

"Yes, and she learned about it recently from Ned Abbott, not from Cooper."

"Really? That's strange. So, did Maya confront Cooper about her songs?" Raul asked.

"I asked her the same question but before I got an answer, a certain Ned Abbott from El Paso sat down at the bar next to her."

"You've got to be kidding me, Charlie! Ned Abbott showed up?" Raul was stunned.

Charlie nodded, "The original songs Maya talked about were a collaboration of, both, Maya and Ned over the years."

"So, what is he doing in Cape Coral?" Raul asked.

"Hard to say, exactly. He claimed that Maya summoned him and he is here to help her out. Not sure with what. But, she said he's here to save his own ass. Again, I do know that Maya was furious with him. And, then, Ned claimed that Maya confronted Cooper about stealing her songs."

"So, what's your take on all of this, Charlie?"

"Well," Charlie shook his head, bewildered, "Maya was boiling over with anger towards Cooper and Abbott. I think she felt betrayed by both of them."

"Do you think she's capable of murder?" Raul asked. "Charlie?" Raul repeated tentatively.

"A couple of days ago I would have said 'no', but now, unfortunately, I'm not so sure," Charlie admitted reluctantly.

Raul scratched his head, "This doesn't look good for Maya. As I already told you, we know she was in Cooper's penthouse the night before he was murdered. And, Ned Abbott? What's your impression of him?"

"A total slime ball. He walked into Slate's and began ordering the bartender around, provoking Maya, insulting me. I couldn't believe it. He called me 'Grandpa'!"

"Oh, really? And, I'm sure you just let that one go, didn't you, Charlie!" Ellen teased.

Charlie cleared his throat and clarified, "Look, I may be seventy-one, Ellen, but I could have kicked his butt. No question about it. And, I let him know that! I, simply, chose not to."

Ellen muffled a giggle. Raul got the picture very clearly. "Sounds like your basic asshole, right? Sorry, Ellen!"

Ellen rolled her eyes. "Really, Raul! I've called people much worse than that myself!"

"So, Charlie, how did it all end on Tuesday?"

"Not very well, I'm afraid," Charlie said sheepishly. "I gave Maya my phone number and she stormed out, yelling at both of us. I think that bridge was burned!"

"So, could Ned have murdered Cooper?" Ellen asked.

Charlie thought about it and declared, "I don't see how. He was in El Paso."

"Well, let's move on. Ellen, what did you learn about Sharon?" Raul asked.

"She sure likes her martinis!" She took a deep breath and summed up Sharon's alcohol-induced confessions. "It took three martinis to get Sharon riled up, but by the fourth one, she was fully-soused and slobbered on about how much she loved Cooper, but he dumped her when he got what he wanted: money. She even talked about their private trysts. But, here's the interesting part. She was obsessed with Cooper and, when he dumped her, she began stalking him."

Charlie was shocked. "You're serious?"

"Oh, yes!" Ellen nodded. "She followed him to Crimson Court, convinced he was seeing some rich lady who lived there."

Raul asked, "And do you know if she followed Cooper on the night he was murdered?"

"I asked her, but she was evasive. Before I could pursue it further, Sharon face-planted into the remoulade sauce." Raul and Charlie guffawed in amusement. Ellen added, "And, on the ride home, she mentioned seeing Cooper in a passionate embrace, late one night, with someone who lived on Santa Barbara Blvd."

Raul made a note of that. Ellen ended her synopsis with one final comment. "Sharon toasted to Cooper's killer, thanking her."

Raul echoed, "Her? She really said, 'her'?"

"That's right, Raul."

There was a knock at the door and, without waiting for an answer, Captain McConnell barged in. He looked baffled as his eyes moved from Ellen and Charlie to Raul and back again. "Swann, I need to talk to you. Now!"

Raul stood up and stepped outside of his office. He returned a couple of minutes later, frowning and shaking his head. He was attempting to absorb this latest information. Ellen insisted, "Raul, tell us what just happened!"

He slowly sat back down at his desk and updated Ellen and Charlie. "We have confirmed that Ned Abbott was not in El Paso on Tuesday, February 26."

"Raul, spit it out! Where was he?" Ellen demanded to know.

"It turns out that he was here in Cape Coral the night that Cooper was murdered."

While Ellen and Charlie attempted to pick up their jaws from the floor, Captain McConnell stuck his head back inside the office door. "And, don't think you can fool me," he good-naturedly admonished. "I know exactly what you, two, are doing here with Raul!"

"Well, Captain McConnell, it's good to know that you're on top of things. I'll certainly sleep better tonight knowing that Inspector Clouseau is on the case," Ellen shot back.

McConnell smiled, tilted his head in her direction, and humbly retreated.

"Well," Raul sighed, looking from Ellen to Charlie. "Let's see. Where were we?"

Charlie smirked, "I believe we left off where Ellen gave Captain McConnell a verbal kick in the butt."

"Oh, yes! That's right," Raul agreed. "Now, we're left with my visit to Frank Blake. Okay, here goes. I got nothing out of him. Nothing! The devoted son was grateful--yes, grateful-- to Stella for all that she did for his beloved mother. He even praised Cooper!" Raul was becoming frustrated. "So, once again, I'm left with this stinging question: how do you, two, do it? Come on. What do you do to get people to talk?"

Charlie spoke. "We both know what Ellen did to get Sharon to talk, so forget it, Raul. Martinis are not part of your arsenal."

"Raul, you're doing the best you can with the resources at your disposal." Ellen added, "Face it, though. You need us. And we won't let you down."

"You, two, are crazy. You know that, right?" They each responded with a nod.

Ellen pointed out, "And, you noticed that Captain McConnell never told us to back off, right?" Raul had to admit that was correct. "So, Raul, just keep doing your job and we'll continue to do ours."

Raul warned, "But only if you proceed with total caution. Ellen, did you hear me?"

Ignoring his question, Ellen asked, "So, when is our next debriefing?"

179

"Monday morning. Ten o'clock."

It didn't take the local police long to find Ned Abbott and bring him in for questioning. He had rented a studio apartment on Coronado Parkway for a couple of weeks. Captain McConnell and Detective Swann were waiting to grill him. They introduced themselves and adjourned to a small, sparsely furnished, windowless room. Ned was seated at a table with Raul seated across from him. Captain McConnell stood, looking down at Ned.

Raul began, "You have been called in for questioning regarding the Cooper, A.K.A. Mark Simmons, murder."

Ned sprawled out his long legs and leaned back in the chair. "I was already questioned by your cronies in El Paso. What's this all about, Detective?"

Raul answered, "Here's the deal, Abbott: I ask the questions and you answer them. Get it?" Ned nodded. "Good. Now, why don't you start by telling me why you're here in Cape Coral."

"Sir, it's a mission of mercy," he claimed. "My friend, Maya Wolfson, called me and needed me to be here for her."

"What do you mean?"

"Look, guys,"

Raul interrupted, "Stop right there, Abbott. You call us *officers*."

Ned mockingly resumed, "Okay, *officers*, I'm sure you already know that she was a songwriter and Cooper was going to steal her songs for his recording deal. Things look pretty bad for Maya right about now since Cooper was killed, so I thought I'd show up and offer her moral support."

"Yeah, Abbott, I'm sure you're just the person she wanted to see," McConnell chimed in. "Now, why don't you tell us the truth."

Ned rocked back in his chair and folded his arms across his chest. "That is the truth, Sir. Maya is looking pretty guilty. I'm an old friend of hers and thought I'd help her through this."

Raul silently glared at Ned waiting for him to sink deeper into a morass of lies. Ned remained silent in return, staring straight back at Raul. Raul decided to cut right to the chase. "Tell me when you last saw Cooper."

Ned slowly lifted his head up and appeared to be contemplating a difficult question. "Hmm, probably about three or four years ago. That would be my best guess," he said smugly.

Raul leaned on his elbows, close to Ned, and said calmly, "Let's try that question again and this time we want the truth. Tell me when you last saw Cooper."

Ned kept his cool and repeated the same lie.

"Now, Abbott, tell me where you were on Tuesday, February 26 between ten P.M. and midnight."

"You're crazy! I was over fifteen hundred miles away--in El Paso, OFFICER!" Ned replied heatedly.

McConnell interjected, "Mr. Abbott, perhaps this will refresh your memory."

At that instant, McConnell slammed a grainy security camera image of a man in profile, on the table. Ned appeared genuinely perplexed and said, "I have no idea who this is."

"We didn't either," McConnell concurred. "But, with the help of our tech team, we were able to I.D. the photo." McConnell slammed a second photo down next to it. The profile revealed a partial view of Ned Abbott's face. Ned stared in disbelief. McConnell bent down and yelled within an inch of Ned's nose, "You're stupid, Abbott! A fancy building on Crimson Court records every person who comes and goes. This photo was dated Monday, February 25, 2019, 5:00 P.M. Now, you better tell us what you were doing in Cooper's apartment the day before he was murdered!"

Ned's defiant slouch suddenly changed as he sat bolt upright in his chair. "This is the honest truth. Cooper phoned me a few days before and told me about his record deal. I figured I'd surprise him and offer my congratulations in person."

"Well, you sure are a man who likes to surprise people, aren't you?" Raul snickered. "Abbott, let me ask you again. Where were you on Tuesday, February 26 between ten P.M. and midnight?"

Ned stammered, "I, uh, I think I was ..."

"Out with it, Abbott!" Raul demanded. "Where?"

"Uh, I think it was The Dek."

Raul slammed his fist on the table and shouted, "And I think you're full of shit!"

"No, Sir, I'm pretty sure I was at The Dek."

McConnell shook his finger at Ned, "Here's the deal. We can't hold you, but we're not finished with you! So, you better stay in Cape Coral until we give you permission to leave. Understood?"

Ned nodded docilely.

"You leave the city, we'll find you and we'll have probable cause to put your ass behind bars, Abbott!" Raul warned.

As soon as Ned Abbott left, Raul made a quick call. "Jennifer, I know I said I'd meet you at the Doctor's office, but it's this damn Cooper murder case," Raul apologized.

Jennifer was trying to be understanding but she was fighting back tears as she spoke. As an ob nurse, she knew that these emotional swings were part of the hormonal changes from pregnancy. But, as a pregnant woman, she wanted to sob and feel sorry for herself. Instead, she, simply, said, "It's okay, Babe."

"Look, call me as soon as you're finished. I love you, Honey."

"Love you, too," she sniffled quietly.

Raul ended the call and walked to the waiting area to escort Sharon Thompson into his office. He was determined to discover what Sharon had witnessed the night of the murder. In general, stalkers make excellent witnesses.

"Mrs. Thompson, please have a seat. Thank-you for coming in on such short notice."

"What's this about, Detective? I've already told you everything I know about Cooper."

"Mrs. Thompson, I don't believe that's true," he smiled politely. "Tell me again where you were between ten P.M. and midnight on Tuesday, February 26."

"I was home watching 'N.C.I.S.' on my iPad," Sharon said disdainfully.

"And, could your husband or anyone else verify this?"

"Detective Swann, I was home alone. Eli and I are not joined at the hip, you know."

Raul leaned forward on his forearms and looked at Sharon straight on. "Mrs. Thompson, let's cut the crap. Since we last met, I've learned that you saw yourself as much more than Cooper's patron, and when he didn't need you any longer, you began stalking him."

Sharon was stunned by Raul's accusations. He had been so deferential on the two previous occasions. Desperate, she dug into her emotional arsenal and could only come up with one strategy to try to deflect this accusation. Sharon broke down and began sobbing convulsively. "You wouldn't understand, Detective. I've felt invisible to Eli for so long now." She paused to blow her nose. "Cooper's success gave me a purpose. I needed to feel important and by helping Cooper succeed," she paused, again, to blow her nose, "I felt valued."

Raul was not taken in by this diversion. "Is that why you felt the need to stalk him?"

"I did nothing of the kind, Detective."

"Did you see him embracing a woman on Santa Barbara Blvd. late one night?"

"That's preposterous! Absolutely not! Detective, when Cooper didn't need me, I understood completely. In fact, I was still planning to hold a fund-raiser for him."

"And, did you follow him on the night of February 26th?"

Sharon's waterproof mascara was worth its weight in gold. With her eye make-up still very much intact, she gazed up at Raul with a look of innocence, and smiled sadly, "Like I said, I was watching 'N.C.I.S.'. Sorry I couldn't be of more help, Detective."

Raul watched Sharon strut away with her head held high. His cell phone rang. "Jennifer!"

"Hi, Babe. All is well. We're having a prune!"

"Whaaat?"

Jennifer giggled, "I mean, our baby, Raul, is the size of a prune. Isn't that fantastic!"

With a sigh of relief, Raul replied, "Oh! I can't wait to see you and the prune. Love you!"

"Love you, too!"

Raul was left to mull over the frustrating interview with Sharon. He, basically, got nowhere. As he reviewed his notes from their previous meeting, he banged his fist on the desk. "Damnit! 'N.C.I.S.'?" The last time he had questioned Sharon, she swore she was home watching 'This is Us' on her iPad.

Thursday, March 21

Charlie's walk to the Boat House this morning was particularly invigorating. The air was crisp and the sky was brilliant. Charlie picked up his pace as he belted out "Zippity Doo Dah". Everyone who passed him going in the opposite direction seemed equally chipper and friendly today. He moved to his left as a runner went by. Charlie recognized him immediately. "Hi, Paul! It's Charlie. Have a good run!"

Paul Shapiro slowed down and greeted Charlie. "I've been hoping to run into you. Want to play golf on Saturday?"

"Of course!"

"I'll meet you at Sunset Bay. Noon. I'll call for a tee time. See you!"

"See you, Saturday," Charlie waved but Paul was long gone.

Before getting coffee at the Boat House, Charlie watched Bud finish up on the racquetball court. Bud let out a howl as his opponent hit a perfect kill shot to win the match. Bud and his opponent shook hands and walked over to Charlie. "Shake hands with my nemesis, Eli," Bud said good-naturedly.

"Congratulations, Eli. That was some shot! I remember you. Bud introduced us at the Boat House a couple of weeks ago. I mentioned that my wife Ellen and I rent a house on Wisteria Court every winter." Charlie was amazed that someone who looked like Mr. Peepers had such a powerful strike.

187

"Oh, yes, I remember you now. In fact, I've met your wife," Eli said. "Wisteria Court? That's not far from here. Which house are your renting?"

"The second one from the corner, on the left. Look, can I treat you both to coffee?"

"Thanks, but I have to be at the office by nine," Eli declined the offer. "See you tomorrow, Bud!"

"Sure."

Bud and Charlie ambled over to grab some coffee. "Bud, Eli's wife is Sharon, right?"

Bud rolled his eyes. "Yeah, I guess so. He and Sharon are like a crocodile and a scorpion. Not sure which is which, but they're a deadly combination."

"The first time you introduced me to him, Eli was ranting that his wife was obsessed with Cooper. Funny, to look at Eli, you'd think he was some mild-mannered patsy."

"Well, not on the racquetball court! Come on, let's get some high-test," Bud suggested. Amy, as usual, brought them coffee before they had a chance to ask her.

Ellen arrived a few minutes later. Stella spotted her and rushed over to whisper something in her ear. "Ellen," she giggled, "you'll never guess what arrived at my door yesterday." Ellen shrugged and Stella eagerly babbled, "A gorgeous, and I do mean gorgeous, bouquet of flowers was delivered with a note."

"How lovely! You must have an admirer."

"No, it's not like that, Ellen. Here, I brought the note with me, hoping I'd run into you." Stella presented Ellen with a small note that read, *"Dear Stella, I am deeply sorry that I had frightened you last week. My mother's death has left a terrible hole in my heart and I took it out on you. You have been a wonderful friend to my mother, and I am grateful that you were part of her life. Please stop by to see me any time Thursday afternoon. I have something of hers that I think she would want me to give to you. Sincerely, Frank Blake 791 S.W. El Dorado Parkway."*

The contrast between the Frank Blake Ellen had confronted and the charming note, gave Ellen a chill as every single vertebrae began to tingle. However, she said, "Stella, that's a lovely note. You're planning to go there?"

"Yes, today, actually. I think it's sweet of Frank to give me something to remember Mildred by."

"Hmm. Very," Ellen replied skeptically. "You know, I don't have any plans today. Why don't we go together?"

"Really? But, Frank got angry with you before. Maybe it's not a good idea."

"Stella, it's a great opportunity for me to apologize for upsetting him. What do you say?"

"I suppose so."

"Great! I'll pick you up at, say, two?"

"Here's my address." Stella wrote it on a napkin.

"I'm looking forward to it. And, oh, by the way," Ellen winked, "please don't mention this to Charlie. Let's keep it between us."

"Of course. Just between us girls!"

Ellen made her way to Charlie just in time to say hello and good-bye to Bud. Bud had to take off because he had promised Karen that he would accompany her to a family reunion this afternoon. "No," he explained, "it wasn't far away. They were going to John Yarbrough Linear Park in Fort Myers." Bud's apparent reticence only served to stir up Ellen's innate nosiness. She found it peculiar that Karen hadn't mentioned it before. Bud answered her questions as if he were being cross-examined by Perry Mason. "Yes, it's sort of a picnic." And, "There probably will be about thirty family members." But, "No, Karen and I don't know anyone who's going to be there." Finally, "For God's sake, Ellen, the reunion isn't Karen's family or my family. It's Clancy, the damn dog!"

Charlie and Ellen roared with laughter. Ellen tried, in vain, to compose herself. "Bud, I remember last year when you used your life savings to pay for Clancy's DNA testing, but a doggie family reunion? Come on, tell us. How did this come about?"

"You know, Ellen, some things are better left unspoken," Charlie cautioned.

Bud was already beyond the point of humiliation, so he explained the origin of this event. "Karen can sometimes get a bit carried away, as you know," he sighed. "Anyhow, she got online and found other dogs in the area with the same DNA as Clancy and decided to organize a 'family reunion' for the gene pool. I made her swear, on Clancy's DNA, not to tell anybody," he muttered, gritting his teeth.

"Well, Bud," Ellen blurted out, "Sure hope it's a h-o-w-l-i-n-g success!"

Once Bud left, Ellen and Charlie took their coffees to a picnic table on the beach. Ellen had brought bagels, strawberries, and the Cape Coral Daily Breeze along with her. She placed the newspaper down and was immediately drawn to the leading headline, "*Person of Interest Named in Cooper Murder*". Ellen read the article aloud to Charlie. "*The Cape Coral Police Department has named a person of interest in connection with the Cooper murder. Ned Abbott of El Paso, Texas had been a long-time acquaintance of the deceased. Since this is an active case, Captain McConnell is not at liberty to reveal sensitive information that could obstruct the investigation. Captain McConnell assures the community that "We are utilizing every possible resource, including our partners throughout the country. Our Department is working day and night to find the murderer and bring the person to justice. While Mr. Abbott is someone the department is thoroughly investigating, he is not considered a suspect at this time. We are, concurrently, checking out several other leads. Anyone with information is urged to contact our special hotline number:239 624-3951."* The article continued on page two with information about Cooper's murder that had previously appeared in the paper.

Ellen couldn't help herself. "Sure hope they're not barking up the wrong tree!" She giggled uncontrollably.

Charlie jumped right in, "It'd be too bad if the tail was wagging the dog!" They, both, were rolling with laughter while they devoured their breakfast.

As they discussed afternoon plans, Charlie began to become suspicious. Ellen, usually quite outspoken, was saying very little. She made a vague comment about needing the car for a couple of hours. Ordinarily, Charlie wouldn't have cared. However, today, he knew Ellen was up to something. She was a terrible liar. But Charlie possessed a quality that must have been surgically removed from Ellen at birth: patience. Therefore, he was perfectly willing to wait for her to decide to let him in on her secret. Unfortunately, Charlie never anticipated that Ellen was about to place herself in danger.

Mangrove Court was a charming street with typical, ranch-style homes backing up to a canal. Stella's front yard was landscaped with palm trees and flowering shrubs. Two large red maple trees provided shade alongside the meandering stone path leading to the front door. Stella was waiting outside her home as Ellen drove up.

Much of the ride to Frank Blake's house was in silence. Ellen found it disturbing that Frank wanted Stella to come to his house to receive something of Mildred's, when all of Mildred's possessions were still right next door. To Ellen, there seemed to be only one logical explanation: Frank Blake meant to harm Stella.

They parked in the driveway and Stella went to the door to ring the bell. Frank answered and invited her inside. As Frank stepped aside to let Stella in, he spotted Ellen. He eyed her suspiciously, blocking her entrance with his beefy body. "Frank, we met before. I'm sure you remember. Ellen Green." Ellen reached out to shake his hand. Frank shook her hand but did not move from the doorway. "May I, please, come in?"

Still silent, Frank stepped aside to let Ellen pass. She and Stella sat down on the Naugahyde couch and Frank sat facing them in a recliner that had seen better days. Stella expressed her appreciation for the bouquet of flowers and gushed that she was glad they could be friends. Frank politely acknowledged her comments and, then, abruptly turned to Ellen. "And what are you doing here? I made it very clear that you are not welcome!"

"Frank, I came to apologize. I believe there has been a serious misunderstanding," Ellen said with sincerity. "Excuse me. May I use your bathroom?"

Frank pointed to the hallway and gruffly said, "Down the hall. Last door on the left."

As she walked down the hall, Ellen could hear Frank say, "She's trouble. I can tell. And you told her about my mother's will, didn't you?"

"Of course not! Cross my heart!" Stella swore. "I promised not to tell anyone about that. And, besides..."

The voices became too faint for Ellen to overhear, so she continued to the bathroom. She flushed the toilet so Frank wouldn't hear her opening the door next to her. Ellen peered in and saw a spare bedroom filled to the ceiling with original paintings, silver serving pieces, cut-glass vases, several chests of drawers--everything but a bed. She knew she shouldn't be snooping, but she couldn't resist. This treasure-trove probably belonged to Mildred. She rummaged around not knowing what she was even looking for, but that didn't stop her. When Stella called, "Ellen, are you okay?" she froze, not knowing what to do. If she answered, Frank would know where she was. If she didn't answer, he would come looking for her. Either way, she was doomed. Ellen decided to do what she did best: take the offensive.

"Stella, I'm coming! I made a wrong turn. How foolish," she giggled nervously.

Frank glared at her with a stony expression. Stella filled in the uneasy silence. "Ellen, Frank has been telling me that he's going to be moving into Mildred's house as soon as the will is probated. We'll be neighbors!"

Ellen glared right back at Frank and said coldly, "How nice for both of you. But, Stella, didn't we come here today so Frank could give you something of Mildred's?"

"Yes, Frank. What was it you wanted me to have?" she asked eagerly.

"Stella, come with me and I'll show you." Turning to Ellen, he ordered, "You stay right here!"

194

Stella followed Frank down the hallway to the spare bedroom. Several minutes passed. Ellen anxiously paced between the couch and the faux wooden entertainment center, imagining Frank choking Stella to death or slashing her throat or clunking her over the head with a cut-glass vase. Ellen was about to grab the table lamp and storm the bedroom when Stella chirped, "Ellen, I'll be back in a few minutes. I'm checking out some paintings!"

Frank returned to the living room and snarled, "We need to talk."

Ellen shot him an imperious look and retorted, "So, start talking!" She plunked herself down on the hard, brown couch and folded her arms across her chest.

"You think you're so smart." Frank spewed, "When you were here last time, you knew all about my mother's will, didn't you?" Ellen waited for him to continue. He began pacing back and forth in front of Ellen, stomping heavily with every step.

Ellen broke her own silence. "I don't know what you're talking about. But, I do think it's strange that you moved your mother's personal items to this place when you're planning to move into your mother's house. Makes no sense to me." Ellen stared at Frank unflinchingly.

"You know exactly why! Cooper. She left everything to Cooper. The house, the furniture, everything!" he sputtered angrily. "I was her only son and I was always there for her but she left me nothing!"

"And how convenient. Now that Cooper's out of the way, Mildred's previous will must be honored," Ellen shot back at him. "Obviously,

195

in a few months, Cooper managed to do what you couldn't manage to do in, what, over sixty years or so?"

Frank's face looked like a pomegranate as he came to an abrupt standstill and stared down at her. At that moment, Stella entered the room carrying a large painting of a vase of daisies. "Frank, I'd like this one."

Frank, magically, became Mr. Congeniality as he calmly said, "That was one of my Mom's favorites."

Stella explained, "Ellen, I never knew that Mildred was an artist. Frank has an entire room filled with her paintings and he let me choose any one I wanted."

"How very thoughtful of Frank," Ellen snarled.

Frank spoke up, "Stella, why don't you wait in the car. I just need a brief word with Ellen. Okay?"

"Certainly, Frank. And, thanks so much! I'm going to hang this in my living room as soon as I get home!"

Ellen couldn't help but notice that Frank, the devoted son, did not have even one of his mother's paintings on display in his own living room.

When Stella got into Ellen's car to wait, Ellen stood up ready to leave as Frank warned her, "Look, lady, I've had it with you and your snooping around! I don't know what you're up to, but I don't like it."

"Well, then, let me tell you what I'm up to, Frank." The more Ellen felt threatened, the more aggressive she became. "I think you had a motive to murder Cooper. That's what I think!"

Frank shook his finger in her face and threatened, "You've crossed a dangerous line and you better butt out, if you know what's good for you!"

"And, you better start coming up with an air-tight explanation of where you were the night Cooper was murdered!"

Frank snarled back, "The last time, you showed up with your bodyguard, lady. You better hope he's with you the next time we meet!"

Ellen shoved Frank aside and marched to the car, shaking in fear. She opened the car door, took a couple of deep, cleansing breaths and sweetly said, "Stella, what a lovely painting Frank gave you!"

Charlie had waited all evening for Ellen to come clean about her afternoon activities. Instead, she avoided being in the same room with him, answered questions with a nod and a polite smile, and, most amazing of all, she agreed with whatever he said. Therefore, the hot tub provided the opportunity for Charlie to get Ellen to open up. He delicately broached the subject. "Ellen, what the hell were you doing this afternoon?"

"My, Charlie! Aren't you the sensitive, new age man!"

"Okay, so maybe I could have been a bit more diplomatic. Let me put it this way: what the hell were you doing this afternoon?"

"Well, here goes, Charlie." Ellen briefed Charlie about her altercation with Frank Blake. When she finished, Charlie's mouth hung open but no words came out.

Finally, Charlie regrouped and declared, "Ellen, this is exactly what Raul told you not to do! We need to contact him tomorrow."

"Think about it, Charlie," Ellen reasoned. "Raul already spoke with Frank and he convinced Raul that it was a simple misunderstanding. And, now, Stella, who was with me, not only didn't feel threatened, she thinks Frank is Prince Charming! Frank has her totally duped."

"That's true, except he's a man with a motive for murder and a temper, who threatened you." Charlie sighed, "Let's talk about this tomorrow." He slid next to Ellen and, protectively, put his arm around her. "And, we can't keep secrets like this from each other, Ellen. That's not okay. Besides, you need to remember that you're seventy-one and stop acting like a little pit bull!"

Ellen relaxed for the first time since the visit to Frank's house. Yes, Charlie was right. From now on, they would be open with one another. No more secrets.

Charlie waited until Ellen was brushing her teeth before bed. He had an important phone call to make and he didn't want Ellen to know about it.

Friday, March 22

A phone call late last night, from Charlie, prompted Catherine to issue a call to action for the Bird-Watchers. One year ago, Catherine, Ted, Karen, and Bud formed the Bird-Watchers. Their purpose was to protect Charlie and Ellen, who had become increasingly reckless as they attempted to solve a murder. The Bird-Watchers, secretly, kept their friends under constant surveillance.

"Karen, it's 9:00 A.M. Emergency meeting, at my place, pronto!" Catherine left this voicemail on Karen's phone. In the meantime, Ted grabbed his bike and raced to the racquetball courts to nab Bud.

After they assembled on Catherine and Ted's lanai and dug into a generous spread of bagels, toppings, and coffee, the Bird-Watchers were ready to be briefed. Catherine wasted no time in getting to the heart of the problem. "Charlie called me late last night. Apparently, Ellen has, once again, gone rogue. She confronted someone she believes could be Cooper's murderer and he threatened her. So, we need to protect her."

Bud took command. "Okay, Bird-Watchers, time for action. Let's get started by reviewing code names. Catherine?"

"Queenie," she replied.

"Ted?"

"Eagle One."

"Karen?"

"Dragon Lady. And, Bud, dear, you need to wipe the cream cheese off your chin," Karen said softly.

"And, Firefly," Bud announced, wiping off his chin. Everyone nodded to confirm their assumed identities. "Now, we know how to tag team and follow Ellen. We are professionals."

"Bud, you're crazy!" Catherine piped up. "We're a bunch of bumbling old farts."

"But, last year we managed to do a fine job!" Karen proudly stated.

"Might make more sense to abduct Ellen until the murderer is arrested," Ted, pragmatically, suggested.

Catherine shot Ted a disapproving look. "Does anyone here want to take responsibility for keeping Ellen in lock-down? It sure isn't going to be me!" They unanimously agreed that tailing her was the less problematic approach.

They formulated their plan, piled right hands on the table, and in unison, yelled a rowdy "WOO-HOO!"

Ned Abbott banged loudly on Maya's door. She was enjoying her third cup of coffee and getting ready to head to the beach for the afternoon. "Maya, open up!" Ned demanded.

"What do you want?"

"I need to talk to you. Open up!"

Maya cracked open the door and, instantly, regretted doing so. Ned pushed his way in and, with a feral look in his eyes, growled, "You realize that the police think I killed Mark or 'Cooper', as everyone here calls him."

"Well, Ned, it looks that way, doesn't it! You made sure that even I didn't know you were in Cape Coral when Cooper was killed. And, now, the police think I was lying and that I'm in on this with you!" Maya shouted. "So, if you didn't kill him, what were you doing in Cape Coral the day Cooper was murdered? Explain that."

"You know why I was here. As soon as Cooper told me about his record deal, I knew what he was up to. Cooper didn't even have the brains to write the lyrics to "Happy Birthday". You and I, both, knew that. So, yes, I went to confront him about it." Ned sat down on Maya's couch, leaning back, with his arms crossed, defiantly.

"Yeah? And how did that go, Ned?" Maya asked, giving him a withering look.

"Cooper, always the consummate gentleman, blamed it all on you, Maya!" Ned accused, raising his voice. "He swore that you convinced him to cut me out of the profit. And, that the two of you were going to make out quite nicely when this album was released."

Maya remained standing and glared at Ned. "You do realize that what he told you was total bullshit, right?"

"No, I believed him. I think, for once, Cooper was being honest. How clever of you to play Cooper and me, each, for a fool. You managed to deceive both of us, Maya! Impressive work! You were

Cooper's sound lackey and you were my collaborator. You managed to build a credible connection with each of us. All those years that you and I sent songs back and forth, I believed in our talent and I trusted you." Ned stood up, placed his hands on his hips and loomed above Maya. "And, now, I see that you're nothing but a two-faced liar!" He, suddenly, grabbed Maya by the shoulders and shook her.

Maya snarled, "Let go of me, you murderous bastard!"

Ned released Maya and, oozing hostility, roared, "I'm not nearly finished with you, Maya!" as he walked out, slamming the door.

Terrified, Maya locked the door and leaned against it, attempting to calm herself down. Tears spontaneously sprung from her eyes. Maya couldn't even remember the last time she had cried. Her first thought was to contact the police detective who had questioned her. She would tell him everything that just took place. But she changed her mind, convinced Detective Swann would think she had something to do with Cooper's murder. Still quivering, she rummaged through her purse and found the scrap of paper with Charlie's phone number. Maya thought he was the one person who might believe her.

"Hello," Charlie said.

"Charlie, it's Maya Wolfson. You said I could call you if I needed to."

"Of course, Maya. You okay?"

"Not really," Maya replied, her voice trembling. "Could we meet? I need to talk to you."

"Yes, I'll pick you up and we'll go to Fathoms. Can you be ready in an hour?"

"Yes, thanks, Charlie. I'm at 436 Santa Barbara Blvd. And, please, let's keep this between the two of us."

"No worries. See you in an hour."

Charlie had no trouble convincing Ellen that he needed the car. Catherine had made it easy. She came through, as he knew she would, and was picking Ellen up to go to lunch at the Boat House. The part about not keeping secrets from each other, well, that would have to wait. But for now, he was all set.

The weather was a bit warmer than usual for mid-March and there was a gentle breeze blowing. Therefore, the beach was teeming with vacationers and locals. Catherine and Ellen walked up the ramp to the Boat House and saw that there were no seats available. So, they strolled out onto the pier and decided to return when the lunch crowd thinned out a bit. As they took in the sights and sounds of the beach, they noticed yellow tape being unrolled from the boat launch, at the far end of the beach, all the way to the Boat House. It appeared that the entire beach was being cordoned off. They asked a leathery woman sitting on the pier if she knew what was going on. She explained that there was to be a candlelight vigil tonight on the beach in memory of Cooper. Thanking her, Ellen and Catherine ambled back to the Boat House to wait.

They found seats fairly quickly. Amy greeted them at their table as she handed them menus. Ellen asked, "Amy, what's this about a candlelight vigil for Cooper?"

Amy rolled her eyes and said, "The police are expecting a mob of old ladies. Excuse me, Ellen and Catherine. I don't mean you! I mean seventy and eighty-year-olds. Really old ladies."

Catherine and Ellen made fleeting eye contact. They decided to take her comment as a compliment. Amy didn't need any prompting in order to continue. "So, I have to work a double tonight and it's going to be horrendous!"

"But why the yellow tape?"

"Oh, I guess you haven't heard. The police are going to be checking everyone. They're concerned that this vigil could become violent like the rally last week."

"And, there's still a murderer out there," Catherine stated.

Amy added, "Yes, but the police think it's that Ned guy from El Paso. I guess they'll be looking to see if he shows up."

"Not likely, Amy. I'm sure he wants to keep a low profile."

"Probably. So, what are you two having today?"

"I'll have the coconut shrimp."

"And the crab cakes for me, Amy."

Ellen was thoroughly intrigued by the idea of a candlelight vigil. It made her feel as if she were twenty once again. And it made her forget all about Frank Blake. It made her feel invincible.

On the other hand, Catherine only had to think back to last week to remember how quickly a peaceful rally turned into a mad rampage. "You're not thinking of going to this, are you?"

Ellen's eyes lit up with excitement. "Catherine, I wouldn't miss it!"

After safely depositing Ellen at her home, Catherine pulled out her radio and transformed into Queenie. "Queenie to Bird-Watchers. Little Package is safe at home. Need reinforcements for tonight."

"Firefly to Bird-Watchers. Explain, Queenie."

"Queenie to Bird-Watchers. Ellen insists on going to a candlelight vigil on the beach. It's in memory of Cooper," she spewed.

"Firefly to Bird-Watchers. Shit! That's going to be impossible to monitor!"

"Dragon Lady to Bird-Watchers. Watch your language, Firefly! And, I know exactly how we're going to pull this off. Meet at headquarters at 6:00. Over and out!"

Charlie pulled up in front of Maya's apartment where she was waiting for him. He was struck by how thin and pale she looked. It seemed that he was always trying to feed her and this time was no different. In a few minutes, they arrived at Fathoms and went inside to be escorted to a table facing the Cape Harbour Marina. Maya ordered the margarita pizza and Charlie ordered the fish and chips.

While they waited for their food to arrive, Charlie spoke up. "What's upsetting you? It's Ned, isn't it?"

"Hmm, how did you guess," Maya said caustically. She decided to tell Charlie almost everything. Maya didn't trust easily, but she was desperate and afraid. She took her time and described her most recent encounter with Ned.

Charlie was concerned and asked, "Maya, do you have a friend who could stay with you?"

Maya shook her head. "If I did, I wouldn't be talking to you, Charlie."

"Well, you need tell all of this to Detective Swann."

"I can't do that."

"Why not?"

"Charlie, I lied to him about a few things. And, he knows I lied."

"What did you lie about?"

"Well, I told the Detective I didn't even know about the penthouse apartment. But, I was in Cooper's apartment the day before he was killed." She paused, "Yeah, I know, that looks really bad."

"Yes, it does. Go on. What were you doing there?"

"Well, I sometimes went to his apartment so we could work on things--you know, work stuff."

"You were there fairly often?"

"Yeah, you could say that," Maya nodded fidgeting with her fork. "I mean, we liked to talk about how to keep doing things better for the next performance and ..."

"Wait, Maya, why didn't you just tell the Detective that? There was no reason to lie. That doesn't make sense," Charlie surmised.

Maya bit her lower lip as she tried to explain, "Well, Charlie, it's--I don't know--it's just complicated. That's all. It's complicated."

"Okay, so here's what we're going to do, Maya. You're going to think seriously about speaking to Detective Swann. You say that he already knows you lied, so come clean with him. In the meantime, I plan to have a little talk with Ned. So, you need to tell me where I can get hold of him. And, I guarantee, he's going to leave you alone." Charlie said, looking intently at Maya.

"Charlie, you don't have to do this for me."

"Oh, yes, I do! Besides, Ned called me 'grandpa'," Charlie grinned. "Can't let that go unanswered."

"Well, please be careful," Maya cautioned. "I'll stay in touch."

When Charlie returned to Wisteria Court, Ellen was reading on the lanai. "Hi, Sweetie!" he called to her.

"Hi! Where have you been?" Ellen asked.

"Santa Barbara Blvd. and Fathoms."

"Santa Barbara Blvd.? What are you talking about?" Ellen asked.

"Actually, I got a call from Maya. So, I picked her up and took her to lunch at Fathoms."

"That's a surprise. It sounded like she blew you off the last time you met."

"I guess, my charm was, simply, irresistible," Charlie winked.

"Yeah, you wish! So, Charlie, what did she tell you?"

"It seems that Ned Abbott gave her a scare. He's blaming Maya and accusing her and Cooper of plotting to cut him out of money for the songs she and Ned wrote together. So, he threatened her."

"He's a detestable bully. Nothing surprising there."

"And, that's not all. Maya said that she had been to Cooper's penthouse apartment many times but lied about it to Raul."

"Well, that wasn't so smart. He already knows she lied."

"Yeah. So, I told her she needs to come clean and contact Raul, but I don't think she's going to."

208

"Maya's putting herself in a bad position if she doesn't!" Ellen concluded.

"I agree. But Maya said, and I quote, 'it's complicated'."

"Well, Charlie, why didn't you say that earlier? As soon as a woman says 'it's complicated', she must be having an affair."

"Ellen, I really think that in this case you're jumping to conclusions," Charlie stated aloud, but to himself he wondered if, perhaps, Ellen could be right about Maya and Cooper.

Before Ellen had a chance to probe further, her phone "can-canned". It was Beverly.

"Hi, Beverly. You okay?"

"Of course, I'm okay. I wouldn't be calling you if I wasn't!"

Ellen rolled her eyes and asked, "Well, then, what is it?"

"I've decided to do you a big favor."

"Really."

"Yes. Am I correct in assuming that you're planning to make a fool of yourself again, tonight, by attending the candlelight vigil?"

"I don't think it's any of your business," Ellen snapped.

"Hah! You're beginning to sound like me, now. Let me get straight to the point. I'm offering to go with you, as your chaperone."

Ellen guffawed at that statement. "You've got to be kidding!"

"I am perfectly serious. And, after seeing that humiliating photo of you in the newspaper, I think you need someone to keep you from getting arrested! Besides, I'm bored and could use a laugh."

"Well, Beverly, hard to turn down such a generous offer. Bring a battery-operated candle and I'll pick you up at 7:00."

"Fine. Later."

Ellen was incensed that she agreed to drag Beverly along. "Why is it I can't say 'no' to that infuriating woman!" she thought to herself.

"Oh, no!" Bud exclaimed. "You're not making me wear that!"

"Honey, it's our only option," Karen assured him. "Besides, you've got the legs for it," she giggled.

Karen presented Plan A, code-named "Daphne". Ted and Bud were going to attend the vigil, incognito, so they could keep tabs on Ellen. The plan was to turn Bud into Daphne, à la Jack Lemmon in heels and a girdle, from the classic movie "Some Like It Hot". Ted was grateful that he had a mustache. That left him wearing a curly-haired wig, baseball cap, Groucho Marx glasses, and a latex nose. But, it was Bud who was, currently, undergoing a dramatic transformation. His impressive cleavage had been stuffed into a shocking pink, long-sleeved blouse. The Vera Bradley wrap-around skirt covered up much of the spandex leggings that he was trying to squeeze into. The topper was his bleached-blond bob with bangs. Karen was finishing up his eye make-up, while Catherine was selecting a lipstick that complemented his complexion.

Bud made one, last, pathetic stab at maintaining his dignity. "Can't I, at least, wear my flip-flops?" he begged.

They all shouted a resounding, "NO!" But, Karen had thought of everything. Earlier, she had stopped at a consignment shop to buy a submarine-sized pair of strappy sandals. "Here, Honey, try these on. They're YOU. And, besides, they match your purse." She had tears streaming down her face by now.

Catherine was biting the insides of her cheeks to keep from whistling as Bud attempted to walk from one end of the lanai to the other. One final sashay across the lanai and Bud's transformation was complete. Ted took Bud's arm and, in a courtly gesture, prepared to escort "her" to the car.

"So," Karen explained, "Ted, you drop off Daphne and," she paused, attempting to sound serious. "And, Daphne, darling, you know what to do from that point."

Catherine called out, "Hey, wait up! One more thing," as she whipped out her phone to immortalize this moment.

Ellen was pleasantly surprised that Charlie didn't put up a fuss about her attending the vigil. He agreed that, with such a strong police presence, the vigil was, probably, a very safe place for her to be. Knowing that the Bird-Watchers were tailing her, Charlie could kick back and watch a March Madness basketball game this evening.

Beverly seemed revved-up as she fastened her seatbelt. "Now, Ellen, remember, you need to stay next to me," she announced. "No disorderly behavior." She shook her finger at Ellen.

They parked near the racquetball courts and headed towards the crowd. Everyone was required to wait in line at a security checkpoint before being permitted to step onto the beach. A disgruntled police officer who appeared to be on automatic pilot grumbled, "Put your arms out to the sides." He wanded Ellen and she was allowed to pass. Beverly was next. At that very moment, a pulsating sound emanated from Beverly's purse. The officer tried wanding Beverly and, while she didn't bleep, the pulsating in her purse persisted. Everyone in the immediate vicinity was focused in on Beverly and her purse. "Ma'am, I need to search your purse," the officer announced.

"Excuse me!" she said in an imperious tone. "You have no right to search my personal possessions. Where is your warrant?" Beverly demanded to know.

"Ma'am, I will say this one more time. I need to search your purse. Please empty everything onto this table."

Beverly reddened as she dumped out the entire contents of her purse. And there, for all to see, was the culprit: a cylindrical, battery-operated apparatus measuring six inches in length. Beverly swiftly composed herself. She looked the officer up and down, put the vibrator back in her purse, and retorted, "I'll take my vibrator over you any day!"

212

The crowd that had surrounded Beverly let out a wild cheer and a round of applause. Even Ellen had to admit that Beverly had been magnificent.

Meanwhile, Ted dropped 'Daphne' off and left her to stumble along, clutching her purse. Nobody even gave her a second glance, which was acutely disturbing to Bud, that was, until he reached the security checkpoint. The officer winked at him and said, "Lookin' good there, babe!" Bud, instinctively, shoved the officer in the chest with his shocking pink purse and made his way through the crowd.

Fully embracing his newly-discovered feminine side, Bud muttered, "Damnit," as he checked out the crowd of women all around him. "I'm way over-dressed!" As he strained to find a sighting of Ellen, he felt himself being pushed forward by the mob. Bud turned around to reprimand the woman behind him and realized, with horror, it was Ellen.

"Sorry!" she apologized without showing any sign of recognition.

Bud effortlessly transposed his voice to a high-pitched falsetto. "No worries, dearie!"

He had never before experienced the sisterhood, but he found it, delightfully, emboldening. Therefore, he joined right in, raising his fist high in the air and shouting, "AGE IS NOT A NUMBER!" And, when the women rhythmically waved their candles in the air from left to right, he waved and swayed along with them. The vigil concluded with everyone holding hands and singing "Michelle". Bud moved his pink purse to his shoulder so that he could link hands with the women on each side. He closed his eyes, raised his chin up high,

213

and belted out a mournful "Michelle". The woman on his right was so deeply moved by his fervor, she began sobbing.

Bud was jolted back to reality when he heard the sound of a car horn honking at him. It was Ted. Bud resentfully staggered and stumbled his way to Ted's car. "So, how did it go?" Ted blurted out impatiently.

"Fine. In fact, I was really getting into it when you rudely honked at me!" Bud protested.

"Well, too bad," he grumbled. By now, his latex nose was itching terribly and he couldn't wait to get home to remove it. "But what about Ellen? Is she okay? Did you keep an eye on her?"

"Now, cool it, Ted. You don't realize what this was like for me," Bud pleaded. "I did my best."

"Bud, your job was to keep tabs on Ellen!"

"I'm sure she's fine. The police are everywhere. Besides, nobody in their right mind would mess with those broads!"

Ted sighed in frustration. "I'll have Catherine call Ellen to make sure she got home alright."

"You won't tell her about my, well, my lapse?"

"I've got your back this time. But, you owe me, Bud!" Raising his eyebrows, Ted teased, "I guess I'm just a sucker for a hot babe like you!"

Saturday, March 23

This was the first Saturday morning since Cooper's murder that the Farmers' Market seemed to recapture its former oomph. Still, a small cluster of women were gathered in the corner where Cooper last performed. They shouted, "ARREST COOPER'S KILLER! ARREST HIM NOW!" However, most of the shoppers scurried around from vendor to vendor, paying little attention to the protesters.

Ellen and Charlie nabbed two almond croissants and were heading to a produce vendor to pick up something healthy to eat, as well, when they spotted Catherine and waved. She was chatting with Sharon. "Charlie, meet you at the tomato guy!" Ellen shouted as she scooted over to Catherine.

Sharon was not looking her usual designer self this morning. Even her oversized Prada sunglasses couldn't hide her puffy face. Ellen assumed that Sharon had already tossed down a couple of martinis by now.

"Ellen," Catherine called out, "tell me about the candlelight vigil!"

"You actually went to that!" Sharon snipped.

"Hi, Sharon! Good to see you. And, yes, I was there. It was moving to see how devoted Cooper's fans are, despite his--er--shortcomings."

"Well, at least, the police finally have a suspect," Sharon said smugly. "I read that he's from El Paso. A Nick someone."

"It's Ned, and he's not considered a suspect at this time," Ellen clarified. "So, that was a lovely day with Pamela, wasn't it?"

"It was pleasant," Sharon glared at Ellen.

"Quite," Ellen said nonchalantly, "And, very generous of Pamela."

"I suppose," Sharon agreed, hesitantly. "Anyhow, Eli still hasn't forgiven me."

Catherine inserted, "For what?"

"Oh, where do I start?" she grumbled, rolling her eyes. "But, I mean, Eli thinks I run my mouth when I've had a drink or two," she explained, turning to look at Ellen.

"Don't be silly, Sharon. You were the soul of tact!" Ellen shamelessly lied. "Gotta go find Charlie before he eats my croissant! Good to see you both."

Catherine called out, "Ellen, wait up. What are you doing this afternoon?" she asked innocently.

"Charlie's going to play golf with Paul Shapiro so..."

"Our dentist?"

"Yes, that Paul Shapiro."

"He really is kinda cute, isn't he," Catherine admitted.

Ellen smiled and raised her eyebrows in response. "Anyhow, I plan to dance around the house all day and eat ice cream right out of the container," she said gleefully.

"Go for it!" Catherine cheered. "Have a great day."

As soon as Catherine ditched Sharon, she made a call on her radio. "Queenie to Bird-Watchers: Little Package is staying in the nest this afternoon. Alone."

"Firefly to Bird-Watchers: I'll stake out the place from 1:00 until 2:00. Eagle One, you're on from 2:00 to 3:00. Dragon Lady, you cover from 3:00 to 4:00."

"Eagle One to Bird-Watchers: roger that."

Karen whispered, "Dragon Lady to Firefly: no way, Firefly! I have a pedicure at 3:00. You figure it out!"

"Firefly to Bird-Watchers: Dragon Lady, ahem, has an emergency. Queenie, I need you to cover her shift." Bud was no newbie at maintaining marital harmony. He was much too smart to get between Karen and her pedicure.

"Queenie to Bird-Watchers: roger."

"Firefly to Bird-Watchers: over and out."

Charlie loaded his clubs into the van and waved good-bye to Ellen. Knowing that the Bird-Watchers were providing constant surveillance, he was eager to try out his new driver. Paul was the first one to have arrived. He was carefully arranging his balls and tees in the front of the golf cart while he waited for Charlie. "Hey, Charlie! Over here!"

"Paul, good to see you." The men shook hands and were soon joined by the rest of their foursome, Mike and Stan. They waited for the starter to give them the signal to tee off and were, soon, on their way.

By the time the foursome finished their round and made their way to the bar on the patio, they were all chatting amiably. Paul began, "So, I read that the police named a person of interest in the Cooper murder."

"Yeah," added Mike. "Some guy from El Paso."

Stan chimed in, "A Ned somebody, I think."

"But what's the motive?" Paul asked.

"I don't think the police have said anything about a motive," Charlie stated.

Paul bought everyone a round of Stellas. Charlie asked the guys, "So, what ever happened to Frank Blake? Doesn't he play with you anymore?"

"Not sure what happened, but he keeps bailing out on us and we keep calling you," Stan explained giving Charlie a pat on the back.

Mike casually replied, "Ya know, I think it's that business with his mother's will. It really beat him down."

Paul just gave a noncommittal, "I agree" in response. He wondered if, perhaps, it was now time for him to contact that police detective and tell him everything he knew about Frank Blake.

Stan piped up, "Yeah, you're right. We should probably swing by his place and drag him out with us one of these days. But, then, we wouldn't get to play with our favorite snowbird!" Stan winked and elbowed Charlie.

The foursome, good-naturedly, teased each other about missed putts, dribbled tee shots, and Charlie's close encounter with an alligator on the fourteenth hole. When they said their good-byes, Charlie got in the van and took out the address Maya had given him. It was time to pay Ned Abbott a visit.

Sharon returned from the Farmers' Market but, before putting away her produce, she walked out onto the lanai where she knew she'd find Eli. "Well, you miserable fool, guess who I ran into at the market?"

Eli glanced up from his Saturday New York Times but said nothing. Sharon answered her own question. "Ellen Green. And, we have nothing to worry about. She said that I was perfectly discreet the other day. So, Swann's questioning had nothing to do with anything I might have said to Pamela and Ellen. In fact, I think it was all speculation on Swann's part and he wanted to see if I was going to take the bait." She triumphantly marched back to the kitchen.

Eli was not convinced. He prided himself on being smarter and more meticulous than most people. So, on Thursday, when Charlie Green, unwittingly, told Eli which house he and Ellen rented, Eli made a note of it. Sharon was full of shit. No way had she kept her mouth shut! Eli decided it was time to pay Ellen Green a visit.

Ellen decided to make pasta primavera with the vegetables she and Charlie had purchased this morning. She would start off dinner with an appetizer of tomatoes, fresh basil, and mozzarella. That meant a bike ride to Paesano's for the cheese and whatever aromas tempted her. Ellen set aside any previous worries about Frank Blake. It was a warm, sunny Saturday--a day that inspired fun not fear.

She was singing and pedaling in rhythm to Carole King's "You've Got a Friend" as she made a right turn onto Coronado. A Porsche, coming up from behind, did the same thing, but cut her off. Ellen slammed on her brakes to avoid crashing into the vehicle. The driver pulled over, opened his window, and stopped. Ellen angrily approached the car. "What the hell do you think you're doing!" she shouted at the driver.

In a measured tone, the driver shot back, "Actually, Ellen Green, I've been following you since you turned off Wisteria. We need to talk."

"Eli!" Ellen exclaimed. "What's going on?"

"Put down your bike and get into the car for a minute," Eli ordered.

Ellen yelled back, "I'm not moving! Anything you have to say to me, you can say right here."

Eagle One was watching this interaction from afar. He began sweating profusely, freaking out that he might have to fight off Ellen's attacker. Nevertheless, he maintained his position, took out his binoculars, and waited. Eagle One was fully prepared to do whatever was necessary. He just prayed that he wouldn't have to.

Eli calmly explained, "Whatever Sharon may or may not have told you and Pamela the other day is alcohol-induced gibberish."

"Oh, really? What are you afraid that she revealed, Eli?"

Eli sneered, "You don't seem to understand. Sharon will do or say anything for attention, especially when she's smashed. So, I'm telling you not to believe a word."

"Well, Eli, she sounded pretty credible to me."

Eli shook his finger at Ellen and said accusingly, "I know that it was you who went running to tell the police what she said! Some detective met with Sharon to question her again. You're nothing but a stupid amateur, butting into something that's way over your head, little lady!"

"Well, little man, I think that you could only be trying to bully me for one reason. That's what I think!" Ellen knew this Melvin Milquetoast was no match for her. She could take him down with her eyes closed.

"You nasty bitch! I'm trying to protect my wife!" Eli yelled.

"Hah! Are you protecting your wife--or yourself?" Ellen barked back at him. Before either one could say another word, a car pulled up

221

alongside Eli and the driver heaved the entire contents of a water bottle in Eli's face.

"Ted? Is that you?" Ellen shrieked with shock.

"You okay, Ellen?" Ted asked, ignoring Eli's face dripping with water and rage.

"Thanks. I'm fine, Ted." For a moment, Ellen almost forgot her manners. "Ted, I'd like you to meet Dr. Eli Thompson."

Eli grimaced as Ted greeted him affably. Ellen cooed, "Oh, Eli, please give my best to Sharon!"

Eli closed his window, peeled out, and left Ellen and Ted howling with laughter. Ted suggested that she put her bike in his car. What a coincidence! He just happened to be heading to Paesano's, too. She was grateful for the ride and never questioned why Ted showed up at that very moment.

Charlie was determined to confront Ned. He banged on the door to the apartment, but Ned did not respond. He asked the desk clerk at the rental office if Ned Abbott was around, but the clerk was busy shopping online for shoes and had no idea whether Ned was there or not. After a frustrating half hour, Charlie left. He decided to return on Sunday and try again.

Much later, once Ellen and Charlie were, both, submerged in the hot tub, Charlie told Ellen about his futile attempt to confront Ned.

Woozy with wine and warm water, she regaled Charlie with her encounter with Eli Thompson.

Charlie concluded, "Well, Babe, you sure kicked his butt!" They both roared over the double-entendre.

"But, seriously, Charlie, Eli was panicked about what Sharon might have said. It's obvious that he was either protecting her or, more likely, himself."

Charlie couldn't resist one more crack, so to speak, at Eli's expense. "I'm sure he was, either, covering his own ass or Sharon's." This comment propelled them, both, into a whole new round of hysterics.

Sunday, March 24

Charlie knew that his best chance of finding Ned Abbott was on a Sunday morning when most people liked to sleep late. So far, Ned had not returned to harass Maya, but Charlie was taking no chances. As soon as he finished eating breakfast, he told Ellen of his plans.

"Charlie, just be careful. Ned could be dangerous or desperate or both," Ellen cautioned.

"Sweetie, don't worry. He's a musician, for God's sake! Who could ever be intimidated by a musician?"

"And, you're a seventy-one-year-old snowbird. Who could ever be intimidated by a seventy-one-year-old snowbird?" Ellen retorted.

"What are you up to?" Charlie asked, changing the subject.

"Page three of the "Style" section," Ellen quipped. "Love you! Bye."

"Bye, Sweetie!"

Ellen had made it to page four when her phone "can-canned". "Hi, Catherine."

"What plans do you have today?" Catherine inquired.

"Making it through every section of the Sunday Times. And you?"

"May go to the Rookery, in Venice, with Ted. He wants to photograph a snowy egret nesting."

"Well, have fun! I'll see you tomorrow for pizza," Ellen replied.

"You have a good day, too. Regards to Charlie."

"Queenie to Bird-Watchers: Little Package roosting today."

"Firefly to Bird-Watchers: we'll do an hourly sweep of the nest starting at ten. I'll go first, then Queenie, Dragon Lady, then Eagle One. Over and out!"

 Ellen's phone "can-canned" again. "Hello?"

"Ellen, it's Sharon. Sharon Thompson."

"Yes?" Ellen said hesitating. "What's up, Sharon?"

"Could we meet? Just the two of us? I need to talk to you."

"I guess so," Ellen stammered. "Where shall we meet?"

"Can you come to my place? Eli's not going to be there. He's got a racquetball tournament in Fort Myers."

"Okay. When shall I come?"

"Right away. Thanks."

Ellen hung up, grabbed a sweater, and rode her bike to Riverside Drive. Sharon was at the front door waiting. They went inside and Sharon led the way to the lanai. "I'll get us some coffee. Please wait here."

Contentedly munching on pretzels, Firefly cruised by Ellen and Charlie's home on Wisteria Court. Everything appeared to be quiet and safe, but Firefly's years with the FDNY trained him to detect the subtlest of changes. That's when he realized that Ellen's bike wasn't parked next to the garage, as it usually was. He spilled the rest of the pretzels all over the front seat as he pulled over and reached for his radio. "Firefly to Bird-Watchers: RED ALERT! RED ALERT! Little Package on bike. MIA. Activate all vehicles. Plan B is in effect! Over and out!"

Ellen surveyed her surroundings and was overwhelmed by the water views spread out before her. To her left was Fort Myers and to her right was the Yacht Club boat dock. However, a nagging feeling of apprehension in the pit of Ellen's stomach cast a shadow over the beauty of this vista. She wondered what Sharon really wanted from her, but was relieved that Eli was not around.

Sharon returned with a tray of coffee and raspberry scones. Ellen felt as if she were being fattened up and lured into a trap.

"Ellen, I'm not one for pleasantries."

"So I've noticed."

Sharon arched her left eyebrow. "Let me get right to the point. What did I tell you and Pamela that day?"

"Well, Sharon, let me get right to the point. What are you afraid you revealed?" Ellen asked, indulging in a lingering sip of perfectly brewed French press coffee.

Sharon hissed, "Stop with the games, Ellen, and tell me what I said!"

"Okay, Sharon. But I'm warning you. This isn't pretty. You told us that you threw yourself at Cooper. He used you for your money and dumped you. Then, you began stalking him." Ellen folded her arms across her chest and waited for a reaction.

Sharon's jaw tensed and she began breathing heavily. "Okay. And what else?"

"I know that you followed Cooper the night he was murdered." Actually, Ellen did not know this but she was feeling foolishly emboldened at that moment. "So, Sharon, what did you witness that night? Tell me."

Sharon placed her elbows on the table and held her head in her hands. She sat in silence, never denying Ellen's accusation.

All of a sudden, without warning, Eli barged onto the lanai. "So, did you end up spilling your alcohol-marinated guts to this nosy broad or not?" he demanded to know.

Sharon yelled back, "Eli, you were supposed to wait in the bedroom for my text!"

"Well, I decided it would be more amusing to surprise you," he smirked at Ellen with a sinister glint in his eyes.

227

Ellen had allowed these two social-climbing degenerates to dupe her. She was furious with herself. She looked around and, wisely, decided to bolt. She made a mad dash for the screen door, ran across the veranda, and charged up the driveway. She hopped on her bike and pedaled hard, never looking back.

It's unfortunate that Ellen didn't look back because, riding down Coronado Parkway, she was being followed by Frank Blake. Frank was whooping with glee at this bit of luck. He was starting to move a few things into his late mother's house and had just finished unloading a car full of his furniture. Stella had greeted him at the back door with a homemade chocolate babka and coffee. She was going to be the perfect next door neighbor!

And, now, the topper: Ellen Busybody Green. "Ah," he smiled, "life--and death--have been good to me lately!" He decided to scare her off for good. Frank pulled up within an inch of the back wheel on Ellen's bike and was about to nudge her tire enough to frighten her. But a car suddenly shot out at him from Monticello Court, missing his passenger door by a hair. Frank stopped immediately and stormed out of his car to confront the driver. Ellen rode away, oblivious to the near collision behind her.

Catherine shot Frank a haughty look as he banged on her window. "Yes?" she said, lowering her window halfway.

"Lady, you almost broadsided me! What the hell were you thinking?"

"I'm thinking it's a good thing I have such quick reflexes, or your car would have been in my way!"

228

"You're crazy! I'm going to report you to the police."

Catherine laughed in his face. "That wouldn't be a smart move. Do you really want to find out if they'll take your word for it or mine? I've already photographed your plate number and am prepared to make a statement."

Frank couldn't believe that his good fortune had turned around so abruptly. He spewed a few expletives at Catherine, stomped back to his car, and drove off in a huff.

"Queenie to Bird-Watchers: Little Package is safe and I need a margarita! Over and out."

Charlie knocked on the door to Ned's apartment and waited for him to answer. Ned cracked the door open, but left the chain in place. "What the hell are you doing here?"

"Open up, Ned!"

Ned removed the chain and opened the door. He was scratching his head and looking slightly disheveled in a tee shirt and a pair of shorts. "Give me a minute to get on some shoes. Wait outside."

A couple of minutes later Ned appeared, wearing a pair of flip-flops. "We can walk to the park over there," he suggested.

"No, we don't need to take a stroll through the damn park together," Charlie countered, blocking the doorway. "What I have to say won't take long."

"Well, then, Charlie, out with it!" Ned shot back.

"You better leave Maya alone!" Charlie glared at him.

"What goes on between Maya and me is none of your fucking business!"

"Well, it is now!"

"You're full of shit!" Ned shouted. "And, just what are you going to do about it?" Ned snickered, placing his hands, defiantly, on his hips.

"You don't want to find out," Charlie warned, shaking his head. He turned to walk away but stopped to face Ned once again."Remember, you're nothing but a punk with a nasty temper, a motive for murder, and an alibi that got shot to hell. I, sure as shit, wouldn't want to be in your shoes right about now!" Charlie turned away, tipped his hat, and strode back to the van. Ned stood in the doorway giving the finger to Charlie's back.

After dinner, Catherine and Ted invited themselves to Wisteria Court. They had disturbing information to share with Ellen and Charlie. A friend of Bud's ran the license plate that Catherine had photographed. Ellen was shocked to learn that Frank Blake was inches away from ramming his car into her bike.

Monday, March 25

"Ellen, you've got five minutes!" Charlie called out.

"I'll be right there!" Ellen's phone rang. It was her friend, Ginger, from Montgomery. "Ginger, hi! What's up?"

"Hi, Ellen. Do you have a minute?"

"I have exactly four and a half minutes. Is everything okay?"

"Everything here is fine. I'm a little concerned about you, Ellen," Ginger explained.

"Me? What are you talking about? I'm great and so is Charlie."

"Well, my friend Laura from Garden Club spoke with her mother Beverly, yesterday."

Ellen was mentally preparing herself for another frustrating visit to check in on Beverly. "Of course, I'll be glad to check in on her for you--for Laura. No problem."

"Ellen, I don't know how to tell you this, but it's not Beverly we're worried about. It's, well, Ellen, it's you." Ginger said cryptically.

"You've got to be kidding, Ginger! I'm absolutely fine!" Ellen's petulant response was really meant for Beverly, but, unfortunately, Ginger was the target.

"Ellen, calm down. Here's what Beverly told Laura. She said that you've been obsessed over the guy who was murdered. You know, the one Beverly had a date with..."

231

"Cooper?"

"Yes, Cooper."

"Well, that's preposterous!"

"Is it really? Ellen, she said that you were on the front lines shouting obscenities at a bunch of old men and..." Ginger tried to disguise her laugh as a cough. She couldn't believe that Ellen was really falling for this.

"Wait a minute, Ginger. Yes, I attended what was supposed to be a peaceful rally that, well, turned a bit chaotic. That's all," Ellen clarified, defensively.

"Ellen, I really wish that were all, but she sent Laura the newspaper photo of you and, well, I'm looking at it right now as we speak. Let me just say, you have looked better!" At that point, Ginger lost it completely. Ellen brushed off her damaged pride and they both had a good laugh at Ellen's expense.

"I can't believe she sent that photo to her daughter! That woman is exasperating, Ginger. You're going to owe me a drink when I get back home!"

"She does sound like quite the character. She said that she had to chaperone you on Friday night at some candlelight vigil to make sure you didn't get yourself arrested," Ginger added.

"Well, I'll bet she didn't tell you the entire Friday night story!"

Ellen was eager to tell Ginger about the pulsating vibrator when Charlie called out, "Ellen, time to go!"

"Sorry, Ginger. I've got to go. Charlie and I have to be at the police station at 10:00. Speak with you later!"

"The police station? What's going on, Ellen?" But, Ellen had already ended the call. Ginger began to wonder if, perhaps, Beverly was the voice of reason, after all.

Captain McConnell was addressing the group assembled in the conference room. Detective Sergeant Raul Swann was seated at one end of the table. Captain McConnell was at the opposite end. The half-dozen detectives in Swann's unit were seated on both sides. "What do you mean that there's no evidence!" he yelled. "It's been almost one month and you've come up with NOTHING?"

"Captain, I wouldn't say 'nothing'. We have a person of interest, Ned..."

McConnell interrupted, "That's a bunch of bullshit, Swann, and you know it. It, basically, means we have no evidence or he would have been arrested and called a suspect!"

"We know he has a motive: he thought Cooper was going to steal his original songs. We can assume he came all the way from El Paso to confront Cooper the night before the murder and, then, lied about it."

McConnell's eyes narrowed and his face turned florid as he spit out, "Find some evidence! This is a murder investigation. Start getting

233

yourselves down and dirty! Find the murder weapon. Ah, hell, find someone else to pin this on, but get me a murderer! The Mayor is demanding an arrest. The newspaper is demanding a press conference. We look like a bunch of Boy Scouts on a scavenger hunt. I've had it with you!" McConnell stood up and slammed the door behind him as he exited.

Raul was left with his unit of disheartened detectives. They had all been putting in twelve and fourteen- hour days in pursuit of this elusive killer. "Officers, let's go over this again and see what we never saw the first fifty times." Raul referred to the flow chart that listed possible suspects, connections with Cooper, motives, alibis. Theories and speculation were thrown around for another fifteen minutes. Finally, Raul concluded the meeting. "Okay, officers, get out on the streets and talk to everyone, anyone. Somebody had to witness this murder! And, always, be safe, be smart, and be thorough. Meeting adjourned."

Raul went back to his office. How the hell was he to begin to move this investigation forward? He seemed to be getting nowhere and, the worst part was, a murderer was roaming about freely. Raul knew that an emboldened murderer meant a murderer who was likely to strike again. And very soon.

Ellen and Charlie were escorted to Raul's office. They were, both, surprised to see Raul looking so glum. He expression was flat. His eyes had lost their mischievous twinkle. He didn't even bother standing up when they arrived. Ellen began, "Raul, you look terrible.

234

It's time to get your butt in gear! We've got a lot to tell you. You ready to listen?"

Raul returned a glimmer of a smile. "Well, Ellen, thanks for your comforting and empathic words. Much appreciated." He and Charlie exchanged a brief look. "So, what have you been up to?"

"Well, Raul, other than being threatened and almost run over by Frank Blake and held hostage by Eli and Sharon Thompson, nothing much," Ellen summed up, offhandedly.

Raul sat at attention and let Ellen continue, which she did eagerly. "Bottom line, Raul, Frank Blake is looking forward to moving into his late mother's home and threatened me when I accused him of having a motive to kill Cooper. Simple as that."

"You accused him of murder?" Raul asked, aghast at Ellen's recklessness.

Ellen shrugged her shoulders and said, "I guess you could say that. I told him that since he had a pretty solid motive, he'd better have a pretty solid alibi for his whereabouts the night of the murder." Ellen told Raul about Frank's attempt to smash into her bike. "And, if it weren't for Catherine, he would have succeeded!"

Charlie added, "Yes, what luck that Catherine happened along!" Raul realized it was more than luck. One look at Charlie's sheepish expression told him exactly what was going on.

"Okay, Ellen. Now, what about Sharon and Eli? I interviewed Sharon last week right after we met. I know she's been lying, but can't pin her down."

"Well, Raul, neither can I. I do know she and Eli were both very disturbed about what Sharon may have revealed to me and Pamela Green. They were disturbed enough to trap me in their home and demand to know what she revealed. I lied and told her that I knew she had followed Cooper on the night he was murdered. But, Raul, she never denied it. She's hiding something and so is Eli. And, it's got to be big!"

Raul was scribbling notes on his pad as fast as Ellen could speak. Then, he said, "Okay, now, let's look at Ned Abbott. He's a liar. We've confirmed that fact. We also know he paid Cooper a visit the day before the murder. His alibi is weak. He claims to have been at the Dek. No one there has been able to confirm it. Charlie, you've been quiet. How have you managed to put yourself at risk since we last met?" Raul asked in amusement.

"I met with Maya. I really don't think she's a murderer. Anyhow, she called me because Ned went to her apartment and threatened her. He accused her of working with Cooper to steal the songs that Ned and Maya wrote together."

"Okay, go on. I know you, Charlie, and I'm very certain that you must have confronted Abbott. So, why don't you tell me what happened," Raul said.

"Raul, I took care of him. He's just a punk."

"Okay, so why didn't you tell Maya to contact me right away if she felt threatened by Abbott?"

"I did tell her, Raul. She promised to think about it. I gather she hasn't called you, correct?" Charlie asked doubtfully.

"Charlie, do you think she could be playing you?" Raul and Ellen, both, looked at Charlie skeptically.

"It's possible, I guess," Charlie said, unconvinced.

Raul sighed, "Here's the plan. You are, both, to back off completely and I mean completely. Ellen, do you hear me?" Raul admonished. "You've made some discoveries that have put both your lives in jeopardy. I am ordering you not to go anywhere alone. And, that means no snooping around! My unit is very capable of following up on every one of these leads. Do I make myself clear?"

They both nodded. "Good! Now, go and enjoy your vacation." They both nodded again. "And," Raul added shaking their hands, "I need to thank you. You've done some outstanding work. I'm hopeful we can, now, wrap up this investigation."

Pizza night was the first chance that Catherine, Ted, Ellen, Charlie, and Karen and Bud had been together since the legendary doggie reunion. Karen may have been sworn to secrecy, but Ellen sure wasn't. "So, Karen, anything special happen last week?" she asked, nonchalantly.

Karen looked thoughtfully at Ellen and said, "Not really. Been a quiet week around our place. What about with you, Ellen?"

Ellen wasted no time. "I've had a crazy week. I feel like I've been running around in circles--you know, *chasing my tail*," she said with particular emphasis on the latter part of the comment. "But, at our age, sometimes we just get *dog-tired*, right Bud?"

Bud didn't look up from his meatball pizza. He silently willed Ellen to keep her mouth shut. But he might as well have willed a yorkie to stop yipping.

Charlie cheerfully jumped right in. "I agree with Ellen. I feel like I've been *working like a dog* this past week!"

Ellen began giggling uncontrollably. Catherine and Ted looked around, totally befuddled by this exchange. Catherine asked, "What have I missed here?"

Bud finally caved. "Okay. It's no big deal. Karen and I went to Clancy's family reunion." He attempted to brush it off casually.

Karen tried to maintain an air of dignity as she described the event in glowing terms. She enthusiastically supplied the juicy details and confessed that the march of the mutts was her favorite part. But it was the family photo she passed around that stole the show.

Catherine exclaimed, "You're serious? Karen, you never even breathed a word of this!"

"Of course I didn't! Bud would've killed me!"

Until this moment, Ted had not said one word, but, he chuckled boisterously, "Don't worry about Bud. His bark is worse than his bite."

As sure as Sharon would have a three-martini lunch, Eli was certain that he and Sharon would, each, be questioned again by Detective Swann. Ellen Green knew way too much and she wasn't about to keep her trap shut. Therefore, Eli realized that he and Sharon could not risk giving conflicting stories to the police. He found Sharon in their exercise room. Eli interrupted her as she was trying, unsuccessfully, to assume the lotus pose.

"Sharon, we need to talk."

"Not now, Eli," she whispered, exhaling loudly, her eyes closed.

"Yes, now!" Eli demanded.

"Damnit, Eli! What do you want?"

They both sat on the bench next to the rowing machine. "Look, we have to assume the worst. Ellen Green is going to run to the police insisting that you told her you followed Cooper on the night of the murder."

"And, what of it?" Sharon said indifferently. "I told Swann I was home by myself watching "N.C.I.S.", or was it "This is Us", on my iPad."

"But, we both know that's not where you were."

Sharon looked puzzled. "How would you know?"

"Sharon, look, this is serious! I know because, Sharon, you fool, I followed you that night!"

"You what! How could you? You swore that you were doing paperwork at the office late that night."

"Well, my dear, it appears that we've both been lying--to the police and to each other. But, that's not the point. The point is, if you killed Cooper, you better tell me right now. We can cover this up. The police don't have any hard evidence. We can pull this off!" Eli grabbed Sharon by her shoulders, forcing her to look straight at him.

"I don't believe you. I think you'd love to see me rot in prison," Sharon retorted angrily.

"You're crazy! I'd be guilty by association. My practice would collapse. My world would be destroyed. I refuse to allow that to happen."

"Your concern is touching, Eli. You just admitted that you were on Crimson Court the night of the murder. How do I know that you didn't kill Cooper?" Sharon shot back with hatred.

Eli's cold, silent stare was his only visible response.

Sharon sat up; her posture was perfectly erect. "So, what if I followed him to Crimson Court? I had too much to drink and knew it. I changed my mind and walked back to my car. But who would ever believe that?"

"No one. Not even me. You look guilty as hell," Eli agreed. "So, you're going to say exactly what I tell you to say to the police and you're not to have even one sip of alcohol until this mess is cleared up!"

Ellen and Charlie decided to take Raul's advice. Today, Ellen invited Catherine and Karen to join her for lunch at Fathoms. Maya was setting up the sound for a jazz group that was appearing there in the evening. However, she had been given the opportunity to sing one of her original songs for the lunch crowd. Ellen was looking forward to hearing her, without any ulterior motives attached. She had decided to leave the detective work to the detectives--at least, for today.

Ellen, Catherine, and Karen were feasting on the portobello mushroom pizza and salads. Their table was alongside the Cape Harbour Marina where they could fantasize about which yacht they wanted to buy. As they finished up their meals, they decided to move to the open-air bar where Maya was due to perform in a few minutes. They paid their bill and brought their coffee with them.

Before she performed, Maya came over to greet Ellen. Ellen was eager to introduce her to Catherine and Karen. She really wanted to know their first impression of Maya. Ellen discovered that she was beginning to agree with Charlie. She couldn't imagine Maya plunging a knife into anyone.

Maya seemed distracted. As Ellen introduced her, Maya's eyes were darting from one end of the patio to the other. Her brows were furrowed and her jaw seemed rigid. Her pale complexion was flushed and spotty. Ellen whispered in Maya's ear, "Are you okay?"

241

Maya attempted to smile and nod in response. Ellen whispered, "Maya, walk with me." Ellen led her towards the marina, away from the lunch crowd. They sat down on a bench. "What's happened? And, don't tell me you're fine. You're not." Ellen was concerned.

"I'll be okay in a minute. Performance jitters, that's all."

"I don't buy that, Maya. Something's very wrong. What is it?" She looked, with intensity, into Maya's eyes. "It's okay. You can tell me."

"It's Paul."

"Paul?"

"Yes, Paul Shapiro, my ex boyfriend. The dentist."

"He's your ex boyfriend?" Ellen was shocked.

"Well, we broke up back in February. Or, I should say that I broke it off. Paul seemed to handle it very maturely. Occasionally, I'd get texts from him asking how I was doing. Then, recently, I started getting voicemails from him saying he wanted to get together--as friends. That sort of thing. I made excuses and now--well, the last week or so-- he's been saying some frightening things."

"Like what?"

"Like, 'Now that Cooper is out of the picture, why don't we start over.' "

"So, you broke up with Paul to be with Cooper?"

"Yes. I guess you knew about me and Cooper? I never told you that Cooper and I were--an item. I never told anybody and, certainly, not Paul!" Maya said emphatically.

"Yes, Maya, I figured out that you and Cooper had been lovers."

"Really? How did you know?" she asked incredulously.

"Let me just say that *it's complicated*," Ellen replied cryptically. "Look, it's not important. But what is important is this. Did Paul know that you and Cooper had been lovers?"

Maya fought back tears and looked at Ellen with her puppy-dog eyes. "Cooper and I tried to keep it to ourselves, but I think Paul found out. He's been harassing me and demanding that we meet. He's sounding like a loose cannon, ready to explode. Look, he knows where I live and..."

"And, what are you trying to say, Maya?" Ellen began connecting the dots inside her head and found them leading to disturbing conclusions. "Maya, tell me. What are you trying to say?" Ellen demanded.

Maya settled herself down and, in a cold, measured tone, looked directly at Ellen and, simply stated, "I'm sure that Paul Shapiro murdered Cooper."

"Paul Shapiro?" Ellen was blindsided. "Paul Shapiro?"

A queasy feeling lingered in the pit of Ellen's stomach. She knew, with certainty, that this murder was one of betrayal and passion. Passion and betrayal. Quite possibly, Shapiro felt betrayed by, both,

Maya and by Cooper, who had posed as his friend. But, equally possible was that Maya felt betrayed by Cooper. They had been lovers and, yet, he was stealing her songs. Or, could Maya be trying to frame Shapiro?

"Maya, you really believe that? You need to tell me!"

Maya inhaled deeply, stood up, and declared, "Yes, I believe that. But now, I have a performance to give." She turned, head held high, and strode to the stage area.

Ellen's heart began to race and her mouth felt like sandpaper. Charlie. She had to call Charlie.

Maya spoke into the microphone. "Good afternoon, everyone. I'm Maya Wolfson, a singer/songwriter. I've been setting up the equipment for this evening's amazing jazz group: "The Cruisin' Blues". They have, generously, offered me an opportunity to sing one of my original songs."

Ellen returned to the high-topped table where Catherine and Karen were seated. Without saying a word to them, she grabbed her phone and sent Charlie a text: "*Charlie, I think Shapiro might be the murderer! Shapiro-Maya ex lovers!*" She pressed "send" and held her breath.

Meanwhile, Charlie was ready to enjoy another perfect Cape Coral day by playing golf. He wasn't able to arrange a foursome, but he was able to get Paul Shapiro to play a round with him. Paul had a rare afternoon free. The course wasn't very busy, so they were able to play as a twosome. They both were playing very well. Charlie was, now, familiar with the course and was able to play more strategically. Paul was hitting his ball a mile. All in all, this was the most satisfying round of golf Charlie had enjoyed since arriving in Cape Coral.

Paul 's drive on the fourth hole was a spectacular shot: long and straight. He walked back to the cart with a swagger. Next, Charlie was about to tee off when he read Ellen's text: "*Charlie, I think Shapiro might be the murderer! Shapiro-Maya ex lovers!*" Deliberately, he shanked his ball into the brush on the right. "Damnit!" he exclaimed aloud. Charlie headed over to look for his ball. This gave him a chance in which to reply to Ellen: "*I'LL FIND OUT!*"

As Maya began singing her haunting melody, Catherine turned to Ellen and asked, "What just happened?"

Ellen whispered, "Charlie is playing golf with our dentist who I think murdered Cooper."

"What the hell are you talking about, Ellen?" Catherine was completely baffled. She got up and ordered Karen and Ellen to leave with her. When they had privacy, Catherine demanded, "Tell me what's going on!"

"Catherine, I don't have time to explain. Charlie could be in grave danger!"

"Well, Ellen, there's only one thing to do." Catherine reached into her purse and pulled out her radio. "Queenie to Eagle One: RED ALERT! RED ALERT! Big Package in danger at Sunset Bay Golf Course. Suspect is Dr. Shapiro. Queenie and Dragon Lady heading there like greased lightning. Grab Firefly and surround them! Pronto!" Catherine turned to Ellen, "Come on, Ellen. You can ride shot-gun."

Ellen was grateful to her zany protectors. But, now, it was time for her to confront Maya. "Catherine, you've got Charlie covered. I need to have a word with Maya. I'll meet you there. Go!"

Maya's song had ended with enthusiastic applause. Ellen approached her, offered her congratulations, and said, "We need to talk." They walked back to the bench overlooking the marina.

"Why are you so sure Paul Shapiro murdered Cooper?" she asked warily.

Maya explained, "I know that he saw us, Cooper and me, one night. We were kissing in front of my apartment and he watched us from his car. I didn't want to believe it was him, but I knew it was."

"Okay, Maya, so he saw you and knew that you had both betrayed him. That doesn't make him a murderer. In fact, Cooper betrayed you, too." Maya nodded in agreement. Ellen continued, "How did it feel to have your lover steal all your years of creativity and cut you out of the deal? Huh? I'll bet that could make you mad as hell! Mad enough to kill!"

246

While he searched for his ball, Charlie was trying frantically to formulate a strategy. He was determined to confront Paul. Without the facts, he had to trust in Ellen's assessment of the situation. She would never have sent that text if she weren't certain. Would she? Charlie found his ball and was able to hit it out of the brush down the middle of the fairway. Next, he surreptitiously tapped the voice memo icon on his phone and, then, pressed the record button. Whatever happened from this point forward, at least he would have a record of it. Charlie took a few deep breaths, straightened up his shoulders, and walked towards the cart where Paul was waiting for him.

Paul teased, "Quite a tee shot, Charlie!"

"Yeah, but at least I recovered," Charlie replied, preoccupied with other matters at hand. As he approached the cart, he could only think of one way to proceed. He would tackle this situation straight-on. He couldn't give Shapiro any room to wiggle himself out of this. "So, Paul, I saw Maya the other day. She's still pretty broken up about Cooper's death."

"Maya? Who's Maya?" Paul asked.

"Paul, really. You know exactly who Maya is. Maya Wolfson, Cooper's sound-tech."

"Well, of course she's broken up about Cooper. She worked for him," Paul shook his head in sympathy. "Come on. Get in."

Charlie climbed into the cart and exclaimed, "Worked for him? Hell, they were lovers, Shapiro! Everybody knew that!"

247

Shapiro clenched his jaw so tightly that the veins in his neck began to protrude. He shrugged his shoulders and replied, "Yeah? So?"

"Wait a minute, Paul. It doesn't bother you? Seriously?"

"It really makes no difference to me. Why would I care?" Paul said dismissively.

Charlie chuckled, "Hah! I think you'd have a good reason to care. Maya broke up with you to be with Cooper."

"Look, Maya and I had split up. It was mutual."

"Really?"

"Oh, yeah. No big deal. In fact, I saw them together and it was pretty obvious. I knew."

"What do you mean?"

Paul said derisively, "Look, Charlie, they were outside Maya's apartment, clutching each other. I happened to be driving by and saw them. Big fucking deal!"

Charlie commiserated, "Well, I'm impressed. You're pretty cool about things, Paul. Maya dumps you for some two-bit con man and you're okay with it."

"Hey, enough!" Paul shouted, turning to face Charlie. Charlie met Paul's glare and stared into two bottomless pools of anger. "Let's drop the subject and get back to our golf game." Infuriated, Paul drove the cart right past his tee shot and the cart lurched forward as he slammed on the brakes.

Charlie ignored Paul's last comment and, scratching his head, muttered, "Paul, I don't get it. There's no way you just happened by Maya's apartment at that very moment. You were stalking her!"

"Charlie," Paul sneered, "You've seen too many movies. I'm no stalker."

"Actually, you're much more than a stalker. You're a murderer, Shapiro," Charlie concluded, dispassionately. He crossed his arms and waited to see what Paul would do. He had dropped the gauntlet and there was no turning back.

"You're crazy, man!" Shapiro's breathing came out fast and heavily. His defiant stare challenged Charlie.

"I may be crazy, but you are a murderer, Shapiro! You were betrayed by Maya and Cooper. You couldn't stand that Maya chose Cooper over you. So, you followed Cooper, intending to kill him. It was premeditated murder, Shapiro! You were played for a fool." Charlie gripped his nine iron so hard, he stopped the circulation in his hand. Then, he waited...

The Bird-Watchers screeched into the parking lot of Sunset Bay Golf Course and huddled together, briefly, to plan their rescue. Firefly took it upon himself to march up to the starter and explain their rather unusual circumstances. He demanded two golf carts in order to track down Shapiro and Charlie. The befuddled starter, reluctantly, agreed when Firefly finally thought to present, what he called, his "Special Ops ID ". He flashed his Paesano's customer rewards card under the starter's nose so quickly, the starter never had a chance to read it. Instantly, two carts were at their disposal.

Queenie and Eagle One took off in one direction. Firefly and Dragon Lady went the opposite way. "Shit!" Firefly yelled. "This damn thing won't go more than three miles per hour!"

Dragon Lady clutched the sides of her seat in terror. "You don't know where you're going anyway. Calm down, Sweetie."

"Yes, I do. I'm following the map," Firefly pronounced in a commanding voice. He squinted, trying to make sense of the map posted on the steering wheel.

Queenie and Eagle One took a different tack. Queenie directed as Eagle One piloted the cart. It felt as if they were moving in a slow-motion video. Queenie screamed in exasperation, "We should dump this cart and start walking. It'll be faster that way."

"Catherine, we don't have a clue where we're going. Be patient!"

Charlie expected an enraged denial from Shapiro. He was not prepared for what happened next. Shapiro began to laugh-- a hideous, bloodcurdling, braying sound. "A fool, Charlie?" Shapiro's nostrils flared. "Cooper turned out to be the fool, after all, didn't he? He thought he could charm his way out of everything--even death." Shapiro shook his head, "But, now I'm going to have to do something about you, Charlie. It's a shame, actually. I've enjoyed our golf together."

"You killed Cooper, didn't you, Shapiro."

"Of course I killed him. I really had no choice, Charlie," Shapiro concluded matter-of-factly. "I did it for Maya. She deserves better--she deserves me. Charlie, I'm sorry, but you've got to be next." With that, Shapiro lunged at Charlie.

Charlie moved so fast to avoid Shapiro's attack, he fell out of the cart. Shapiro cackled loudly as he aimed the cart straight at Charlie. Even at top golf cart speed, a direct hit could prove perilous. Charlie scrambled to the nearest shrub and dodged the cart.

"Shapiro, you bastard, you may be stronger and younger, but I've got my nine iron!" Charlie yelled with ferocity. He swung wildly at Shapiro with his trusty nine iron.

Shapiro shifted the cart in reverse, switched into forward, and took off at a brisk three miles per hour, abandoning Charlie. "Damnit!" Charlie grumbled, as Shapiro fled the scene. Charlie sent off a text to Ellen: "*HE DID IT! NO QUESTION!*"

Ellen had just accused Maya of murdering Cooper when her phone honked--a text from Charlie: "*HE DID IT! NO QUESTION!*"

"Oh, my God! Maya, look!" Ellen showed Maya the text. Ellen's eyes welled up with tears as she frantically tried to call him back. No response. She texted. No response. "Maya, I have to call Raul."

251

She called the emergency number and waited. Unfortunately, Raul's voicemail answered. "Raul, Ellen Green. Charlie is in danger! He's at Sunset Bay Golf Course with Paul Shapiro. Shapiro murdered Cooper. Charlie may already be dead!"

"Ellen, come with me," Maya ordered, taking Ellen's hand. "My car is over there. Let's go."

"Maya, I'm so sorry. I shouldn't have..."

"Forget about it, Ellen. Charlie needs us!"

Back at police headquarters, Detective Raul Swann listened to a message from Ellen Green. He was totally baffled by her accusation. Paul Shapiro? Paul Shapiro, D.D.S.? That wasn't possible! He held his head in his hands as he carefully listened to the voicemail again to be sure he had heard it correctly. If he shared this information with Captain McConnell, McConnell would consider it nonsense. But what if Ellen were right about Shapiro?

Raul banged on McConnell's office door and barged in. "Sir, you need to listen to this voicemail. It was left on my phone ten minutes ago."

"This better be good, Swann. I've got important matters to take care of."

"Please, Sir. Listen to this now," Raul pleaded.

When McConnell finished listening to the recording, he leaned back in his chair and asked Raul, "So, what do you plan to do about this?"

"I'm going straight to Sunset Bay. I'll need back-up."

"That damn Green woman! She sticks her nose into police business and could get herself killed and, worse than that--she pisses me off! Go! Now! And take Decker with you."

"Yes, Sir."

"And, one more thing, Detective."

"Yes, Captain?"

"Be careful. You're going to be a father pretty soon."

"Yes, Captain." Raul nodded, summoned Sergeant Decker, and was on his way.

If ever Charlie needed a lucky break, it was now. "Please," he pleaded to no one. Charlie worked as a ranger back home and knew that the ranger carts could go three times faster than the golfers' carts. If he could track down a ranger, he could easily beat Shapiro to the parking lot. Just this one lucky break and he vowed never to become impatient with Ellen again. He vowed to listen to Mozart without complaining. He vowed to schedule the colonoscopy he had put off scheduling.

And, luck was with him. In the distance, he saw a cart with one man in it. He began running towards the cart, madly waving his hat in the air. He was sure that this had to be a ranger. The rangers were all retired men, like Charlie, looking for some part-time work and free golf.

"Hi! Need a lift?" asked a jocular man with silver hair.

Charlie tried to catch his breath. He knew that what he was about to say would sound preposterous. "Look, I'm Charlie, a fellow ranger."

"Charlie, pleased to meet you. I'm George." They shook hands. "So, what's up?"

Charlie got right down to business. "I know this is going to sound crazy, but the guy who murdered Cooper is heading to the parking lot in a golf cart. I know we can overtake him in your cart."

"Whaat! And I thought I had heard just about everything. But this is a new one!"

"Listen, he's the guy who killed Cooper! He's wearing a red shirt, white hat. You've gotta believe me!"

"Well, Charlie, my wife would kill me if I were responsible for letting Cooper's murderer get away. So, hop aboard and hang on!"

Fortunately, the ranger wasted no time. He got on his two-way radio. "Alert. All rangers. Find a solo driver: red shirt, white hat. And surround the cart! I repeat. Find a solo driver: red shirt, white hat. Surround the cart. Driver is desperate and dangerous! I repeat: driver is desperate and dangerous. Full speed ahead! Over and out."

Seconds later, half a dozen rangers swarmed the golf course and attacked every possible route in hot pursuit of Shapiro.

In the meantime, the Bird-Watchers were flailing about at a frustrating pace. Eagle One, always camera-ready, spotted a lone cart with a lone driver nearing the eighth tee. Eagle One zoomed his lens in on the driver and passed the camera to Queenie who nodded to confirm Shapiro's identity.

Catherine whispered into her radio, "Queenie to Dragon Lady: perp on the eighth tee. We're closing in." They painstakingly made their way along the edge of the course, slowly inching their way to Shapiro. Firefly and Dragon Lady were chugging along back at the third hole.

A vigilant ranger spotted a solo driver wearing a red shirt and white hat. He transmitted this message to his brothers: "Alert. All rangers. Solo driver with red shirt, white hat approaching eighth tee! I repeat: solo driver with red shirt, white hat approaching eighth tee! Full speed ahead!" In no time at all, they formed a wide circle around Shapiro's cart, blasting their storm-warning horns to attract attention.

Shapiro bolted from his cart and attempted to flee on foot. However, the rangers were skilled pilots and swiftly closed in on him. They shoved Shapiro to the ground and immobilized him. Charlie was awarded the honor of tying him up.

At the same time, the rangers' storm-warning horns alerted Raul and Decker. They ditched their cruiser in the parking lot and charged up the fairway.

Ellen and Maya pulled into the lot and raced towards the action, not too far behind Raul. Ellen was in a frenzied state. She envisioned Charlie being rolled down the hill in a body bag.

Instead, what they witnessed was a formidable sight. A silver-haired posse had formed an impenetrable circle at the eighth tee. In the middle of the circle was Dr. Paul Shapiro with his wrists securely bound together. He vehemently denied Charlie's accusation and, instead, took the offensive. Shapiro bellowed, "I've been attacked by a demented lunatic!"

In response, Charlie let his cell phone do the talking. He pressed "play" as Shapiro's voice was heard loud and clear: "Of course I killed him. I really had no choice, Charlie..."

Ellen, Charlie, and Maya spent the next several hours back at police headquarters being debriefed by Raul and Sergeant Decker. When they were permitted to leave, Ellen and Charlie invited Maya to join them for dinner. She thanked them but was too emotionally drained to think about food. Maya had been through a horrendous day. She just wanted to go home and try to sleep. But first, she promised herself, she needed to call Ned and tell him what happened. Still, for Maya, the most painful part of this ordeal was the fact that, in spite of everything, she truly loved Cooper.

Ellen and Charlie hugged Maya and wished her a good night's sleep. They turned to say good-bye to Raul. Captain McConnell was standing next to him. Raul nudged McConnell forward and uttered a loud "Ahem! Go on!"

McConnell cleared his throat and said, "Thank-you, Charlie and Ellen Green."

"Well, Captain McConnell, we're always happy to do what we can to ensure that Cape Coral continues to be a safe, crime-free community," Ellen said with a wry smile as she reached out to shake his hand.

Charlie shook McConnell's hand and nodded, "Our pleasure."

McConnell paused for a moment. He looked baffled. "I don't get it. How the hell did you figure out that Shapiro did it? He wasn't even a suspect."

"Maybe it's because people share things with us that they turn around and forcefully deny as soon as the police start hammering them with questions. We're the wacky older couple--a bit zany but totally harmless," Ellen summed up.

"Yeah, right!" McConnell scoffed. "You, two, are anything but harmless!"

"Well, then, Captain McConnell, it must be that we outsmarted all of you--once again!" Ellen winked and, with a flourish, paraded out the door.

Wednesday, March 27

The lead story in the Cape Coral Daily Breeze and the Fort Myers News-Press was about the arrest of Dr. Paul Shapiro, D.D.S. for the murder of Cooper, A.K.A. Mark Simmons. A mug shot of Shapiro was juxtaposed with a flattering photo of Cooper, his captivating smile in full view. Shock-horror spread throughout the southwestern gulf communities.

The articles concluded with a shout-out to the silver-haired posse that apprehended Shapiro. Mayor DeLisi, Police Chief O'Leary, along with Captain McConnell and Detective Sergeant Raul Swann, were planning to honor these heroes at the Yacht Club beach tonight at sunset. The public was cordially invited to attend.

Preparations for the sunset celebration began by noon. A staging area was set up, decorated with banners, flags, and flowers. A sound system was wired to accommodate microphones and live music. Crowds began gathering by late afternoon. Toddlers, teenagers, adults, tourists, business owners, began swarming the beach. But, most notably, an immense gathering of women of a certain age began arriving in vans, Corvette convertibles, limos, on foot, in wheelchairs, and even in buses.

Ellen, Charlie, Maya, and the Bird-Watchers were driven by limo to the beach. They were given V.I.P. passes so they could be seated in the first row, facing the staging area. They eagerly greeted Raul's wife, Jennifer, who was seated with them. Families of the silver-haired posse were seated in the next two rows. The program began with the Cape Coral high school choir singing "The Star-Spangled Banner" just as the sun dipped below the horizon. This was followed by a local Eagle Scout leading everyone in the "Pledge of Allegiance".

The Mayor stood at the podium. "I'd like to give a heart-warming welcome to everyone here. By the size of this crowd, I am reminded of what a special community we are here in Cape Coral." A loud applause and cheer followed. "The Cape Coral Police Department has demonstrated incredible dedication and professionalism in making such a timely arrest in the brutal murder of Cooper. Thank-you, Chief O'Leary, Captain McConnell, Detective Sergeant Swann!" Each man stood to acknowledge a boisterous cheer from the masses.

"Without further ado, I would like to present a Certificate of Appreciation to each of our heroes who put their own lives at risk in order to apprehend a dangerous murderer," Mayor DeLisi announced with pride. "And, to give our heroes the welcome they deserve, I'm thrilled to present Cape Coral's hottest sensation, Signal III, right here on the stage with me!" The crowd went wild as the Mayor gestured to the band. This talented group is made up of five Cape Coral police officers and one sheriff's deputy. They had been headlining shows to sell-out crowds throughout Southwest Florida for almost two years.

Right on cue, Signal III rocked the stage with the rousing 1980's song "Celebration". A procession of golf carts rode in triumphantly, towards the beach, from Driftwood Parkway. The silver-haired posse made their entrance waving their Sunset Bay Golf Course hats at the crowds and beaming with pride. Everyone seated sprung to their feet, dancing, cheering and clapping along with the music, until their palms were red. Woohoos, hoots, whistles, shrieks, from the massive crowd drowned out any remarks that immediately followed.

The six golf rangers had won the hearts of the entire community. They ascended the staging area where they formally accepted their well-earned honor. Each ranger shook hands with the dignitaries on the stage: Detective Sergeant Swann, Captain McConnell, Chief O'Leary, and, finally, Mayor DeLisi. The silver-haired posse bowed to acknowledge the overwhelming support of this spirited throng. Then, they, each, directed their gaze to the gutsy golfer seated in the front row. And, in unison, they tipped their hats to Charlie.

September 28

Six Months Later

A murder has an insidious way of touching lives: the lives of those closest to the victim as well as the lives of those who never even knew the victim. And, the Cooper murder was no different. Its impact reverberated throughout the community and far beyond, forever changing the lives of many.

Dr. Paul Shapiro was found guilty of murder in the first degree. He was sentenced to life-without-parole in a maximum-security prison.

Beverly Miller was proud, but not the least bit surprised, that her tennis team took first place in the Soledad Country Club Championship. Recently, she flew up North to visit her daughter, Laura. Unfortunately, Beverly neglected to remove the battery in her vibrator prior to going through the security check. Ever unflappable, Beverly, grudgingly, submitted to the "pat-down" before being permitted to board her flight.

Ned Abbott returned to El Paso one month after the arrest of Dr. Shapiro. He and Maya took the time to collate all of their original songs and agreed, in writing, to share both the profit and the credit with each other as they pursued their individual careers. Before leaving Cape Coral, Ned humbled himself, perhaps for the first time ever, and apologized to Charlie for referring to him as "Grandpa".

Frank Blake waited until Mildred's will was officially probated before completely moving into his mother's home. Always one who knew on which side his bread was buttered, he remained very attentive to Stella, who lived next door.

Stella Reynolds was thoroughly delighted with her new neighbor, Frank. She baked him a chocolate babka, without fail, every week.

Sharon Thompson and Eli Thompson continued to treat each other with hostile indifference, but thousands of miles apart. Sharon checked herself into the exclusive "Wala-wala-kiki Spa" on the island of Maui where she gave up martinis and became a Buddhist. She posted on Facebook, to her water aerobics class, that she is planning to remain there indefinitely and is, currently, cohabitating with the thirty-nine-year-old owner of a head shop. Eli continues to be an ass.

Detective Sergeant Raul Swann and Jennifer became the parents of a beautiful, seven-pound baby girl on September 15. They named their daughter Charlene Eleanor.

The Cooper Senior Music Studio Fund actually became a legitimate, charitable, 501C3, organization. Cooper's devoted fans chose to honor his memory. Money has poured in from all over the area, including Fort Myers, Sanibel, and even Naples. Cooper may have been scamming his fans, but these women received a priceless gift in return. He made them feel beautiful and sexy. Sure, Cooper had his flaws, but, what the hell, nobody's perfect. The generous funding enabled the board of directors to purchase and renovate a building not far from the Cape Coral Farmers' Market. Above the main entrance to the building is an inscription, "AGE IS NOT A NUMBER".

Maya Wolfson was the logical choice for executive director of "The Cooper Senior Music Studio". In addition to her many responsibilities, Maya is in the process of finalizing a recording deal. The album will feature original songs she created, many in collaboration with Ned Abbott.

Catherine printed eight by ten glossies of the photos she snapped the night of the candlelight vigil: Ted arm-in-arm with Bud who appeared in all his feminine glory. She and Karen plan to make the photos into a Christmas card collage to send to Ellen and Charlie, who had absolutely no idea to what lengths the Bird-Watchers would go to protect their dearest friends.

Ellen and Charlie both had to admit that during the Cooper murder investigation they had, each, behaved recklessly at times. They agree that they need to start acting their age. But, well, perhaps, not yet. Maybe next year...

Notes

This book is a work of fiction. Therefore, most of the characters are creations of the author and, in no way, represent real individuals. However, several of the characters have been inspired by real people whose names have, mostly, been changed. They include the following:

Catherine and Ted

Karen and Bud

Hugh and Ginger

Bob, the bartender from Slate's

Colleen, assistant manager at the Boat House

Jay, manager at the Boat House

Amy, server at the Boat House

Pamela and Ron Green, owners of the Westin Cape Coral Resort at Marina Village

Ruth, owner of Maria's Pizzeria and Restaurant

Rory, server at Maria's

Rose, owner of Paesano's Italian Market and Deli

Captain J.R. Tremper, owner of Banana Bay Tours

First Mate Andy

Signal III

Ellen and Charlie Green

The following restaurants, listed alphabetically, are local favorites:

Bert's Bar and Grill

Boat House Tiki Bar and Restaurant, Cape Coral

Boat House Tiki Bar and Restaurant, Fort Myers

Fathoms

Maria's Pizzeria and Restaurant

Marker 92

Merrick's Fish Tale Grill

Nauti-Mermaid

Redfish Grill

Slate's Restaurant and Sidedoor Jazz Club

The following are real places/points of interest, listed alphabetically:

Antique Barn at Water Street Market

Banana Bay Tour Company

Barbara B. Mann Performing Arts Center

Cape Coral Farmers' Market

Cape Coral Resort at Marina Village

Mount Dora Antique Extravaganza

Paesano's Italian Market and Deli

Six-Mile Cypress Slough Nature Preserve

Wisteria Court house

Yacht Club beach

Brief history of Cape Coral:

Cape Coral is a friendly, laid-back city located on Florida's gulf coast, just west of Fort Myers. It was founded in 1957 by Leonard and Jack Rosen, real estate developers, who envisioned Cape Coral as a planned residential community. As a promotional campaign, some of the model homes were actually given away as prizes on TV shows such as "The Price is Right".

Today, Cape Coral is a thriving residential and business community. In fact, it is the largest city between Tampa and Miami. The four-hundred-mile canal system gives boaters easy access to the Gulf of Mexico. Bicycle paths, parks, beaches, and nature centers offer residents and visitors a wide variety of outdoor activities.

Carol and her husband, Bill Freeman, grew up in Gloversville, NY and, currently, reside in Montgomery, NY. Carol has enjoyed being a snowbird in Cape Coral, Florida since her retirement in June 2015. She and Bill spend much of their time with their three grandchildren and their antique business and plan to never act their age.

Prior to retirement, Carol worked as a school psychologist. She is the author of two previous books about parenting. Bill had a long career in sales and marketing. Together, they owned and operated a very successful bed and breakfast for ten years. They bring their combined professional work experience, energy, and can-do attitude to every new venture upon which they embark.

In close collaboration with Bill, Carol is also the author of *The Cape Coral Caper: Murder on the Caloosahatchee.*

56633583R00156

Made in the USA
Middletown, DE
23 July 2019